■ □ ■ □ ■

GAPS

■ □ ■ □ ■

WRITINGS FROM AN UNBOUND EUROPE

Gaps

A Novel

BOHUMIL HRABAL

Translated from the Czech
by Tony Liman

NORTHWESTERN UNIVERSITY PRESS
EVANSTON, ILLINOIS

Northwestern University Press
www.nupress.northwestern.edu

This book is published with the support of the Ministry of Culture of the Czech Republic.

Printed in the United States of America

10 9 8 7 6 5 4 3 2 1

Library of Congress Cataloging-in-Publication Data

Hrabal, Bohumil, 1914–1997.
[Proluky. English]
Gaps : a novel / Bohumil Hrabal.
p. cm. — (Writings from an unbound Europe)
Translated from the Czech by Tony Liman.
ISBN 978-0-8101-2550-6 (pbk. : alk. paper)
I. Liman, Tony, 1966– II. Title. III. Series: Writings from an unbound Europe.
PG5039.18.R2P7613 2011
891.8′635—dc22

2010050770

♾ The paper used in this publication meets the minimum requirements of the American National Standard for Information Sciences—Permanence of Paper for Printed Library Materials, ANSI Z39.48-1992.

The grotesque is the absolute comic.

Charles Baudelaire

■ □ ■ □ ■

GAPS

■ □ ■ □ ■

And the advance copy of my husband's first little book was so long in coming that he wasn't even drinking anymore, at night he just ranted he was going to jump out the window, throw himself under a train, so on my second day off I dressed in my fanciest outfit, slipped on my red high heels, grabbed my little parasol and set off for the publishing house. And there I stood before the editor-in-chief and told him who I was and pointed my parasol in the direction of Libeň, to number twenty-four Na Hrázi Street, and said . . . Now look here, somewhere up there is that jewel of mine, he's not even drinking anymore, doesn't even have the strength to throw himself under a train, all because the advance copy of that famous little book of his is taking its sweet time . . . Go see for yourself what you've done to him! And I stood there in my mascara stood there in the first position of dance my little red shoes turned out and shining, and the editor-in-chief was rattled and he picked up the phone and made a call and when he hung up he told me the advance copy was definitely on the way . . . but I said, I know it's on the way, but by the time it gets here that jewel of mine will have kicked the bucket, I'll go and get it myself . . . now tell me, where exactly is *Pearl of the Deep*? And lo and behold the editor-in-chief himself says, I sympathize, before my first book of poetry came out I couldn't wait either, I was throwing myself under trains and thinking the most desperate thoughts . . . And he picked up the phone again and presently a clerk brought in that advance copy, the advance copy no publisher is ever supposed to part with.

So I left the publishing house and strode along National Avenue and I had a patisserie wrap up that copy of *Pearl of the Deep* for me, wrap it in tissue paper and tie it with ribbon like it was a little present . . . And I walked down Wenceslas Square with pride, parasol in one hand, *Pearl of the Deep* tied in red ribbon in the other, I strutted along daydreaming how beautiful it will be when this little book comes out and that jewel of mine and I stroll this same square together and see *Pearl of the Deep* in the display case window of the Kniha bookstore, and I'll throw a party, an in-house wedding, with champagne flying like my husband just took the Formula One . . . And then I got an idea, I walked over to Spálená Street, to the paper salvage where my husband baled old paper under the electric lights for four years, and I stepped into the office and there was the boss, the woman who'd drummed out my husband, and the personnel screener, the guy who'd called my husband a slacker because he got a grant from the Writers' Union literary fund to write part-time . . . and I untied the red ribbon and showed them the blue jacket and mainly I showed them my husband's name . . . and I said . . . feast your eyes, my husband *is* a writer, despite the crow you made him eat . . . And I wrapped up *Pearl of the Deep* again, retied the red ribbon, and out I went to the courtyard, where I turned and held that parcel up to the window, and there they sat, dumbstruck, because this they hadn't expected . . .

The windows of our flat on Na Hrázi Street were flung open, and squatting on the doorstep like a giant bald-headed bird in an aviary was Pepíček, he smoked and wore those spectacles of his that looked like two jam jars, and somehow my husband was up and around, washing dishes . . . I walked in and set that little parcel tied in red ribbon on the table, next to two shot glasses and an open bottle of rum . . . Guess what it is, I said . . . But my husband went on washing dishes and said . . . I know, but to suppress one's excitement is noble! Look here, Pepíček and I have agreed, as soon as you're off to your brother's in Vienna, we're going to paint not just the rooms white, but the doors, windows, and chairs too, brighten up this black humor of mine . . . And tiny Pepíček came in and those jam jar spectacles of his glinted and threw reflections around our flat and Pepíček said . . . Doctor, one more shot . . . and he held up his glass and it glinted just like those spectacles . . .

My express train to Vienna was scheduled to depart in fifteen minutes, and as I stood on the platform my husband ran up toting a mesh shopping bag, he seemed drunk again, but it was intoxication from his little book, his advance copy, and he helped me into the carriage and hollered . . . What a triumph! Twenty thousand copies printed . . . and now they have to unwrap every last one of those packages, seven editors they have to proofread and they missed a typo anyway! Imagine! The text reads . . . an NSU Sport *Marx* with a silver hood lay in the gutter . . . And what it should read is . . . an NSU Sport *Max* with a silver hood lay in the gutter . . . Seven women forced to go through twenty thousand copies just to retouch the . . . *r* . . . ! And wrap everything up again into packs of twenty . . . ! that jewel of mine shouted and I was mortified . . . For God's sake, keep it down . . . And the conductor blew his whistle and my husband got up to go and now everyone in the compartment stared in disbelief . . . That mesh bag of his brimmed with hundred crown notes . . . And the conductor whistled again and my husband stumbled to the platform with his mesh bag, it looked like he was carting home a bunch of spinach . . . and the train began to pull out and my husband trotted alongside my window and explained . . . They gave me an advance of ten thousand crowns . . . Pepíček and I are going to paint the apartment . . . and then he stood there swinging his mesh bag, hundred crown notes shining like spinach . . . When I sat down, the woman seated opposite said . . . Your husband is quite the cheerful fellow, I'll wager the fun never stops, eh!

The express eased into Franz Josef Station, I stood in the corridor and outside on the platform was my brother Karl, Karli . . . When I descended from the train with my valise Karli was already coming toward me and we rushed into each other's arms and embraced, could it really be, Karli and I . . . together again after all these years. When I could finally see through the tears, there he was, as elegant as ever, decked out in the finest clothes and finest shoes, an immaculate shirt and carefree necktie. His hair was a little thinner, but still chestnut and wavy, and he was scented with cologne and the scar on his chin lightly powdered, the scar he took from a grenade fragment somewhere out on the Eastern Front . . . Then we loaded my luggage into the trunk of his Simca and that Simca was as spit and polish as my brother's shoes, as my whole brother was in fact, whom I hadn't seen since the end of the war, couldn't have, because Papa, all those years ago, was against him spending time with his Czech friends, his Czech girlfriends, he wanted Karli to devote himself to our plywood and veneer business, but Karli preferred to go out dancing in Prague with his pretty girls and his friends . . . And so he drove me through Vienna in that Simca of his, made a point of driving me down Kärtner Strasse and Mariahilfer Strasse, and I was struck by those wide avenues and beautiful shops and by all those people stepping out, free to go about their business, and we drove along in a rush of traffic and somehow Vienna seemed grander and more beautiful than I remembered her, back in the Břeclav days when my girlfriends and I skipped school, played a little hooky, and caught the express train to Vienna . . . but all that was at the beginning of the war . . . And soon we arrived in the Vienna suburb of Radaun where my sister-in-law welcomed me and I recognized instantly that it was she who kept Karli in shipshape, she who made all the decisions, not just at home but everywhere . . . she was a pleasant woman, sort of the Vienna type, shaped like a bowling pin, and she smiled, but it wasn't a pleased-to-meet-you smile, in fact my sister-in-law only lightened up when I said I was just here for thirteen days, and then it was back to Prague, because Prague was now home . . . and I could just see the weight drop off her shoulders, and she laughed, delighted I was not planning to stay in Austria for good . . . Meanwhile Karli slipped off his shoes and gave them a quick buff with a flannel cloth before changing into his slippers, I too had to take off my shoes and I sat in the living room with the door to the kitchen wide open, the kitchen was all white, like at the dentist's, and my sister-in-law donned a white apron and proceeded to prepare dinner, she sat on a white bar stool decked out in chrome trim, went through white enamel cupboards filled with an array of colorful spices, and the carrot and parsley she was chopping shone with freshness . . . and then she brought in a plate of veal scaloppini . . . and Karli inquired softly was Prague still as beautiful as she had been back when he was young, when he went to college there and played for the school tennis and basketball teams? And did they still have dancing at The Little Heart and the Ball Negre? And how about the Juliš arcade?

And the Vltava dance hall on the first floor? And did they still hold the men's eight rowing races? And when I told him I worked as a waitress at the Palace Hotel Grill, he lit up and asked was the food there at the Palace Hotel still as wonderful as it used to be . . . ? And so I lived at Karli's place in Radaun, and evenings waited for him outside the factory, as late as five thirty he was still running across the courtyard of that Vienna woodworks in his white smock, it was a good thing Papa wasn't around to see it, Karli could have taken over the reins of Papa's company, but he'd been too busy running around Prague with his friends and his beautiful girls to show any interest in Papa's firm . . . Karli probably knew in advance how everything would come out, in the end Papa lost it all, because the last thing he expected was for the Germans to lose the war . . . When Karli drove me to Salzburg he showed me the beautiful villa Papa could have bought back in '34, but why, since he owned an even more beautiful villa in Hodonín, but of course Papa could not have foreseen how it would all end, not just for him, but for the whole family, even Liza and Uncle Wulli . . . And so every day Karli and I set out for someplace new, we went to the Hotel Sacher, and to Tallern for chicken, and then the Café Deml, where the shop girls addressed us in the third person . . . *Was wünschen Sie sich?* And then Karli and I went to the Café Hawelka, and to Grinzing, and we drove down to Klosterneuburg, and strolled along Kärtner Strasse and the Graben, and I was dazzled by Vienna and her shops and her lovely Viennese German, and it made me heartsick, I thought if I had the chance to start my postwar life over again, there's no place I'd rather be than Vienna, it was like being home again, everyone here reminded me of the people I'd lived with up until '45, because my mother had been Austrian, the daughter of a chief forest ranger, but the more smitten I was with Vienna, the more my sister-in-law poured cold water on the idea, that was all well and good, she said, but Vienna was all work, work, and more work, she herself had to toil in that shoe factory until six o'clock every day . . . and Karli said . . . But I'm an outsider here, Vienna never took me in, my life in Vienna consists of going to work and coming home again, a little TV, and then it's early to bed so I can get up in the morning and go to work and slog away again until five thirty . . . I'm an outsider here, the only thing is I'm free to go wherever I want on my holidays, swim in any ocean, ski wherever I want at Christmas . . . But in this city I'm an outsider, a Sudetenlander, though my most beautiful years were spent in Prague, with my Czech friends and Czech girls, Prague was home to me right up until Hitler came, Mama went to see him too when he rolled through Vienna, I remember she wept at the luck, and Liza and Auntie Pišinka cried those same tears of joy, Auntie Pišinka who died last year, but I knew right away it was all over with the girls in Prague, with my Prague friends . . . and because we lived in the Sudetenland we were Germans and I was sent to the front . . .

I was returning to Prague from Vienna a little wiser. I stood at the window of the Vindobona Express in tears . . . Karli was on the platform looking up at me, he'd bought me a new ensemble and a whole suitcase full of clothes and little gifts, my sister-in-law held my hands and gave me a little smile, she was exactly the type of woman Karli needed, not an ounce of feeling, nothing fazed her, she knew what she was about, and she also knew that without her Karli would collapse . . . And then the whistle blew and the express started pulling out and Karli cried and dabbed at his eyes and at his chin with his handkerchief, my sister-in-law wore a little smile that said she was glad I was returning to Prague, glad she'd have some time to relax after my visit, and the last thing I saw was Karli lean over and lightly dust off his trouser leg with his handkerchief and then the tips of his shiny shoes . . .

My husband was waiting for me at the Prague station, hungover, he didn't even give me a kiss, and I pulled away from him because he reeked of beer, he smiled sheepishly and carried my bags and because there were no taxis to be had we took the tram and I looked out at Prague and saw she really was a mess, scraps of paper everywhere, half the buildings wrapped in scaffolding, downtown Prague was starting to look like the outskirts, construction trailers, piles of boards and I-beams fenced off with barbed wire, and for the first time I realized that if not for this mess, the center of Prague would look just like Vienna . . . And it seemed my husband was part and parcel of everything I saw in those streets, it dawned on me that he was even like that on the inside, that he thought like that, and dressed like that, he was just like those slapdash streets and squares of Prague . . . And when we got off the tram and rounded the corner of that little street of ours

I practically fainted, only now I noticed how ramshackle and dilapidated all those houses and buildings were, peeling paint, every second building missing its gutters, the street full of garbage . . . And then I was enveloped by the damp hallway and the cold coming from the yard, and Mrs. Beranová had the water faucet open wide and splashed bucket upon bucket on the checkered floor beneath her window . . . with her straw broom she swept the water into the drain and by way of greeting said . . . Don't even tell me where you were! You know I lived in Hamburg for twenty years . . . ! And I continued up the stairs and there it was! Doors and window frames gleaming white through the wild grapevine cascading from the roof . . . and I smiled at my husband . . . and even inside in the half-light everything shone white, the chairs, the table, the walls . . . and the advance copy tied with red ribbon was still there just as I'd left it. I kissed my husband on the cheek and asked . . . So what's going on? And my husband said . . . *Pearl* came out yesterday and it's already completely sold out . . .

Pepíček passed away . . . from the enamel paint fumes and the endless procession of rum shots tossed back with my husband, the same Pepíček who could always be found squatting on a Libeň bench or at Mr. Vaništa's or at my husband's side. A week went by before they found him there in his flat on Slovanka, abandoned and alone, for his relatives lived somewhere in Canada . . . and Mr. Vaništa the barkeep informed the appropriate authorities that he would shoulder the expense of the funeral himself . . . So there we were in the small parlor of the crematorium, Mr. Vaništa brought his guitar along, and there was the coffin and a sign that read who was inside the coffin . . . JOSEF SVIATEK . . . and my husband paled and said to me, You know, I never knew Pepíček's last name was Sviatek . . . and then an attendant appeared and simply read what was on the obituary . . . and then I placed a single flower next to the coffin, and Mr. Vaništa took up his guitar and bowed to Pepíček Sviatek, and then he propped one foot on the step and strummed several chords and began to sing Pepíček Sviatek's favorite song . . . Girl from the Rowhouse with the Beautiful Smile . . . Mr. Vaništa sang with the same passion as when he sang O sole mio down at the pub in that tenor of his that reminded one of Benjamino Gigli . . . So beautifully and with such feeling did he sing Girl from the Rowhouse that other attendants came through the parted black velvet curtain to listen . . . while the coffin made its way slowly behind the partition . . .

What happiness when my husband brought his author's copies home by taxi, what joy! And he bought sixty more copies for himself and unwrapped them right away and placed them side by side like he was laying tile, and I just couldn't believe my eyes that that jewel of mine could be so childish. And then he signed every single one of those books and forced me to cradle one in my arms like a newborn, he said that's the way it's done, that Vítězslav Nezval demanded his lovers cradle the poet's newborn babe, be honored by it, because, as that jewel of mine told me with a tear in his eye, a writer's real children are his books, he's not just the father to those books but the mother as well, in fact he's even more than a mother, because a writer, and now my husband pointed to himself, to his stomach and his head, a writer carries that future book of his for more than nine months, and just like a mother feels it growing inside of him, moving and kicking, and just like a mother worries is the child going to turn out all right? Will it be able to make its way in the world . . . So my husband blathered on and those books of his were all laid out across the floor and I just rolled my eyes and said . . . Seriously? You've got to be kidding . . . Are you sure you're feeling right in the head? Who would've believed it . . . And just in case something does come loose, which asylum shall I tell them to take you to? Beřkovice or Bohnice?

And so the first debacle came to pass . . . My jewel went to the bookstore there on National Avenue for the book signing and he wore a beautiful suit made for the occasion and he was decked out with a necktie and his readers crowded round the table while a young woman, most likely a salesclerk, held each book open for my husband to sign, and my husband looked every one of those readers in the eye and asked kindly what they'd like him to write, and then he scrawled his signature and was moved by the whole thing, not like he was pleased with himself, more like all that admiration made him weak in the knees, and he sat there and he really did remind one of the son of the rabbi from Nikolsburk, and I stood in the corner and peered out from behind a book of poetry, I hid behind the book of poetry and eyed my husband like a detective, watched that jewel of mine perform his shenanigans, but he seemed sincere, like just then he had confidence in himself and in those readers of his, for whom he wrote his *Pearl of the Deep* . . . at home when I flipped through the book it certainly was a far cry from something like Mr. Škvorecký's *Cowards* or *Nylon Age* and I'd trade every one of those stories in *Pearl of the Deep* for just one story by Mr. Chekhov . . . but what threw me were those readers who looked at that jewel of mine in awe, they even blushed and stammered in his presence, so excited were they at the chance to see and hear the famous writer . . . And so as the line in front of the bookstore grew, so too grew my husband's confidence, he was all smiles now, no longer the nervous wreck . . . my husband could only be himself in those Libeň pubs of his, the moment we entered some restaurant where people were well dressed and behaved accordingly and engaged in polite conversation, my husband paled and seemed confused and stammered and blushed, and he only came to his senses once we were back outside—polite company gave him the sweats something awful . . . But here, during the book signing, where he was unrestrained by etiquette, where he was surrounded by well-behaved people who all felt inferior to the great writer . . . here my husband behaved as he would at Mr. Vaništa's, as he would at The Old Post . . . And then the salesgirls locked the front doors and outside still more readers pounded on the glass, but in vain, it was six o'clock and the last signatures went to those inside . . . That jewel of mine got up to go, and same as when our wedding ceremony wrapped up at the Little Château, he reeked of beer and brandy . . . he had dark circles under his eyes and deep lines around his mouth, he waved and thanked the manager, even kissed her hand . . . And we exited by the back door, the keys rattled in the lock behind us, and I strode alongside my husband and smiled to myself, strode along in those red high heels of mine keeping time with the tip of my parasol, and I just had to smile because it was only yesterday that my husband, when he looked ahead to the book signing, was puking like a dog, he didn't get a wink of sleep, and akin to our wedding he shouted he wasn't going, and in the event he was, they'd have to drag him there with a plow, like a miserable mean ox to the slaughter . . . and now he strode alongside me, full of himself, it was obvious that jewel of mine even thought everyone we passed on National Avenue recognized him for the great writer, and with a nod of the head he returned greetings that weren't even there . . . and right out of the blue, just before he pulled me into Pinkas for a pint, there in the crowded street he raised his arms and shook his fists and shouted . . . You're the man! You did it! And then he invited me into Pinkas to celebrate, and we stood at the taproom bar, and my husband ordered me a pint while he himself chugged one beer after the other, just about as fast as the waiters could sling them off the pewter bar . . .

So I say, Mother, I can't believe it, I looked at that famous book of his, but when I read it I got the sense every reader should finish it off at home, like those prepared meals I buy, the ones I have to finish off, tweak a bit, add spice to so they're whole . . . Mother, though we spoke German at home, I did have Czech schooling . . . it seems those short stories of his are off somehow, like curdled milk, what do you think? And that's just what she was waiting for . . . Well, sweetheart, you're pretty much right, look here, grammar school and even high school he always had C's and D's in grammar, he flunked his first and last years of middle school, and among his other D's he always flunked Czech language . . . whatever he touched, darling, that son of mine messed up, at ten years old he started cutting out these decorative pieces with a coping saw, with an eye to making little cases or a box for a hairbrush and the like . . . but he could never put them together . . . and then he got into stamp collecting, I bought him an album, he had a whole box of rare stamps he'd found in the attic . . . and what do you think he used to glue those stamps into that expensive album . . . ? Gum arabic! First he brushed some onto the bottom of the stamp, and after sticking it in the album, he went on to brush not just the whole page with gum arabic, but everything else, himself, us, the table, not to mention his hair sticking to his pillow . . . so said Mother with a laugh . . . Or the time he got into bookbinding . . . followed the handbook and everything . . . stretched some string out on a frame, cut those sections into pages carefully . . . and then he went at the sewing, all cross-eyed, tongue hanging out . . . and then it was time to make the covers . . . and again glue everywhere, everything stuck together . . . and when he tried to fit and bind into the covers what he'd sewn together . . . it didn't even line up . . . Therefore, darling, nothing at all surprises, that writing of his bears the style of all those mistakes of his all that clumsiness! Why, he could never solve a single crossword puzzle, a single rebus, a brain teaser in the newspaper, he just went red in the face and stopped right up . . . Ach, and then when he was a young man he decided to give photography a whirl . . . and when he emerged from the bathroom spattered with fixer and developer . . . not even one photograph turned out . . . and on the off chance it did, it looked like it was shrouded in smoke . . . Or when spring came he took up gardening, he had all these rocks and alpine flowers . . . ach, the care he gave it, the bruised fingers, the slaving away until he built that rock garden . . . and in two months it was all gone . . . swallowed up by dirt and weeds! Darling, from what I'm telling you here you can form a picture of that jewel of yours, as you call him . . . When the Germans closed the universities he attended Eckert's business school . . . And you know what, try as he might he was the only student who couldn't learn shorthand! Typewriter was the only thing he could write on . . . Or when he was a dispatcher, that sonny of mine was the only one who couldn't get the hang of the telegraph, much to the amusement of everyone else . . . The piano too, with those stubby fingers of his, not that he couldn't play, he could even handle Liszt and Chopin . . . he wanted to play, but those stubby fingers of his stumbled across the keyboard . . . Playing alone he could still get by, but as soon as someone stood behind him or looked at his fingers that's all she wrote, he just went red in the face and gave up . . . About the only thing he was good at was hard physical work, during the holidays he always helped bring in the harvest, carried bags of grain from the thresher to the granary at Doctor Sedláček's, who had a farm in Zálabí and a manager and ten women to help in the fields come harvest time . . . and here my sonny the university student excelled, here he worked for his pay, here everyone sang his praises, here he was on his game, because he was made of tough stuff, and that he was, hard physical labor was his thing, one doesn't have to think when at that sort of work, and when he got his pay he put back awful amounts of rye liquor, everywhere he went a shot of rye liquor, and when he drank at the Pub Under the Bridge he even played piano there, Strauss waltzes, even had the sheet music . . . but when it came to hard physical labor . . . Same thing in Kladno, same thing at the paper salvage, same at the theater, four years at each job, and do you know the only reason why, darling, he worked himself to the bone? Because he didn't know how to do anything else . . . And now that he's gone through all the possibilities, everything he could easily have been number one at, Bang! He turns into a writer . . . Darling, it's a slapstick comedy, I don't believe it myself, but I see it with my own eyes, read about it in the papers, that sonny of mine, hang onto your hat, is on the verge of becoming a bestseller! Can it be possible! No, it can't! But as we see, it is possible, and then you're going to tell me there are no miracles in this world . . . I'm afraid he'll go on to publish even more books, because readers today are awfully perverse . . . Who reads Galsworthy? Or Artsybashev? Or Jirásek? But Hrabal! He's our scribe . . . So said mother and she laughed and clapped her hands . . . And I say, Mother, how can he possibly be a writer when he can't even fill in a form properly? Sure he'll fill it in, but late, after he's supposed to, and then it's all wrong anyway . . . Where it says given name he puts his surname, where it says surname that jewel of mine puts his given name, he writes his nationality in the wrong place, signs his name where the clerk's stamp is supposed to go . . . every time they give him hell and when I deliver those forms myself . . . I always come back red with shame, every single application I've got to go back and forth five times . . . And mother laughed and nodded agreement to everything . . . And I said, Mother, even this you find amusing?

And so I recalled those golden days when my husband had no money of his own, when he was happy for the little potfuls of food I brought him from the Hotel Paris, with a spoon he'd wolf down the sauerbraten, the steak, the goulash at midnight . . . now I remember how I always wanted someone to steal that advance money that he toted around in his mesh shopping bag, but of course no one thought my husband was packing tens of thousands, they just figured it was old lotto tickets or something, my husband wandered the streets and alleys and avenues of Prague with that mesh bag of his, and when he went into a pub he simply hung that bag brimming with thousands of crowns up on a coat hook.

Now my husband changed not just his bars and pubs, but his friends as well, he spent generously on beer, paid everyone's round as long as it was beer, it was hard to get him into a wine bar, and if you did it was never for very long, he had to have a pub, it wasn't the beer itself he was crazy about, but rather the gossip, the raucousness, the drunks carrying on, in short, he liked everything about it that I didn't . . . I could last about an hour before my head started to spin, not from the smoke and fumes, but from that crazy palaver my husband held so dear. Now he liked going to Pinkas and he liked going to Varous across from Czechoslovak Writer, and now it was a different group of friends he hung out with at the Golden Keg, and across the Vltava he went to meet friends at the Olympia for more of that pilsner beer of his, and I joined him there once and met some of his new friends, I took a shine to Mr. Linke right away, the very handsome gentleman who edited my husband's books, and then there was Mr. Ducháček, a diminutive drunk who kept a journal where he tallied his daily beer consumption, he showed it to me at the Olympia, fifteen thousand pints in five years . . . Mr. Ducháček was a folksy sort of fellow, but when he tied one on he liked to pick fights with men twice his size, he'd stand up, fists at the ready, but in the end Mr. Ducháček was usually able to restrain himself, to spare the giant . . . And then there was Mr. Karel Pecka, a pleasant gentleman whose thick hair was cut very short, like he was just out of prison, at least that's what it looked like to me, and sure enough Mr. Pecka had spent fifteen years in the lockup, he was just starting out with his writing, and when my husband read his first short stories he immediately took them down to the publishing house, to Mr. Ducháček and Mr. Dostál . . . And sunlight shone through the windows of the Olympia, it was quite a pleasant restaurant, and all my husband's friends were in good spirits, in an unusually fine mood, my husband had that advance of his stuffed into the mesh shopping bag, fifteen thousand crowns in one hundreds, and it really did look like he was carting a few kilos of spinach around, and every fifteen minutes or so another round of beer arrived, and then someone walked in and there in the open doorway sang in a beautiful tenor . . . *We're off to Maxim's to have us a gay old time* . . . and a bespectacled gentleman walked over to our table, they introduced him to me as the painter Mikuláš Medek, and the barmaids came over and welcomed him with the utmost respect, they cooed over him and asked what was his pleasure and Mikuláš Medek ordered himself a vermouth . . . and one of the barmaids asked . . . and what else, Mr. Medek? And the painter ordered a soup bowl as well . . . And the barmaid smiled . . . And what is that for, Mr. Medek? And he said . . .

Something to let a little puke into . . . At which point I got up to go, and said my good-byes, the only one I shook hands with was the very handsome Mr. Linke and then I was off . . . only later did I learn that the painter Mikuláš Medek had diabetes, and when he took a drink of vermouth it was only a matter of time until he started to throw up, hence the soup bowl . . .

So in fact I got caught in my own trap. Somehow the offer I made to my husband, that I'd look after everything while he stayed at home and wrote, backfired, and the plan lasted for all of about half a year. After which he needed neither those little potfuls from me nor the occasional fifty crowns pocket money, in fact he had so much money of his own it left me speechless. And along with his newfound success, which I didn't expect, came travel abroad. Once he went on a bus tour of Austria with a group of writers. I went to see him off, Mr. Kolář was going too, and to me all those poets really did look like poets, except for my husband, who in their midst looked like an ex-footballer, or a farmer.

And then he traveled to England, and then to France, and then to America, where he struck up a friendship with the writer Arnošt Lustig, who to me didn't look like a writer either, he had thick curly hair and skin as beautiful as a young lady's. I was absolutely floored to learn that Arnošt had spent almost six years in the concentration camp at Terezín, an ordeal that started for him when he was sixteen years old, he didn't like Germans, and as my husband told me, never spoke a word of German . . . Arnošt knew what to eat to look after himself, whereas my husband, as I could well imagine, wolfed down everything given him . . . In Paris they lived at the Hotel New York across from the Saint-Lazare railway station, they were always famished before lunch and dinner, particularly my husband, who apparently was fond of devouring all the rolls and all the mustard even before the soup and appetizer came, and at the end of the day I'm glad I never accompanied him on any of those trips, I would have died of shame if I had to sit at the table with someone as uncouth as that jewel of mine. When he arrived in London, there at the airport a group of workmen was moving a piano, and my husband broke off from his own group and made to direct those men on where to go, until he led those gullible fellows right down to the basement, while the grand piano should have gone up two flights to the restaurant on the second floor, and the workmen came looking for the group from Czechoslovakia, intent on giving my husband a thrashing, and the writers from Prague got a big kick out of it, while the Slovaks bawled my husband out for so poorly representing Czechoslovak writers . . .

I heard that Arnošt Lustig, when his kids make such a racket he can't write, buys a basketful of oranges and bananas and chocolates and other goodies . . . and he brings it home and gathers his kids around and points to the basket and says . . . Look here, Daddy needs to write and you're making a racket, if you stay nice and quiet, you'll get this whole basket of goodies . . . And why will you get this basket? Because when Daddy writes he makes money, but if you're going to keep screaming like a bunch of banshees, Daddy won't be able to write and then do you know what you'll get? Shit. And there was the story of how Mr. Lustig bought himself a little cottage in Roubíčková Lhota, a place where he could write when the kids were acting up and those baskets of goodies were in vain. When Mr. Lustig finally sat down to his typewriter at the window so he could write without interruption in the peace and quiet of Roubíčková Lhota, a detonation rang out and the cottage shuddered . . . but Arnošt persevered with his writing, until finally he was so on edge from those explosions that the prospect of working at home, even with the kids raising hell, was like a dream . . . So he went outside, in the direction of the explosions, and a short distance from the cottage he discovered a granite quarry newly opened, and he asked the workers, How long is all this going to be here? And they told him it was granite for building a new highway and there were two shifts going at it. And Arnošt said with a smile . . . And how long do you plan on quarrying this granite here? And they said, not long, only about ten years . . . My husband liked to say that he never met a happier person than Mr. Lustig, or a more pleasant companion . . . they always shared a room together, whether it was Paris or New York, and my husband told me that all the stewardesses were head over heels in love with Mr. Lustig . . . In Paris my husband could hardly sleep a wink, always up at first light thanks to the din coming through the open window from nearby Saint-Lazare station . . . and first thing in the morning already there were two stewardesses perched on Mr. Lustig's bed, brushing his thick curly hair, and they were honored to brush the writer's hair, to engage him in conversation, and Arnošt lounged there for a while and then strolled around in his pajamas, plump, well rested, as if he'd never spent a moment in a concentration camp, quite the contrary, as if he'd lived his whole life in the lap of luxury. And in New York Arnošt took my husband around to all those Jewish friends and acquaintances of his, there in New York they published not just his novels, but his short stories as well, and when my husband woke up, there was Arnošt, still asleep, surrounded by his editors, who lounged by his bedside and smoked and waited for Arnošt to wake up so that they might speak to him, so that they might sign him to a contract, not just for the books he'd written, but for the books he was going to write . . . And Arnošt, when he woke up, said to my husband, Hey, you dirty whore, today we'll drop in on Elia Kazan, and I'm going to buy you, wherever you like, a can of the greatest beer around . . . And so that jewel of mine covered just about every inch of New York City with Arnošt, he told me about the time they were coming out of their hotel on Twenty-eighth Street, suddenly to hear gunfire, and there were the cops, Colts drawn, firing down the stairs into a subway station, from where unseen shooters fired back, and people scattered in all directions or threw themselves on the ground, something straight out of a movie, and along comes Arnošt, all done up, hair coiffed, and he steps over to the police officer, who's crouched by the subway entrance with his pistol aimed downstairs, and with a light tap on the shoulder Arnošt says . . . Excuse me, could you tell me where the nearest mailbox is?

Then there was the time my husband sent me to his mother's place to pick up a bushel of early pears, already bought and paid for in Nymburk, and Mother and I sat around while I went on at length about everything that was happening, not that I was complaining, since everything I dished to Mother with respect to my husband only made her laugh anyway, but the upshot was that along with those pears Mother gave me a little tabby kitten to take back, and she said if this little kitten, this little tabby, doesn't work on my husband, there's nothing much left that will, because all those years he lived at home there was nothing he ever loved more than those cats, those little kittens. And so I brought that kitten home, and when my husband returned from his trip abroad, when he laid eyes on that kitten, he didn't even ask about the pears, and then I saw a side of him that was entirely new to me. He was thunderstruck by that little kitten, he went all soft and gooey, he brought milk right away, and when the kitten was done lapping it up my husband made a little bed for it in a box, and then he brought in an old sink and filled it with sand, and that night he didn't go anywhere, he just sat there watching the kitten, petting it, holding it up and gently pressing it to his cheek, he claimed that a kitten like that could chase away stress and sorrow, that a little tabby like that was capable of great feeling. And he let me draw back the covers for him and like a shot he was off to bed, taking that kitten with him, the kitten snuggled up to him but because my husband's breath reeked of beer it turned away, and so my husband got up and brushed his teeth and then the little kitten snuggled up under his chin and fell fast asleep, my husband couldn't get the smile off his face, and that kitten suckled at his finger, the skin on his knuckle, and then my husband, who couldn't stand it if I happened to brush up against him at night in bed, slept all night long in a completely unnatural position, the kitten snuggled up to him, suckling gently at his knuckle, and that jewel of mine, kitten sleeping sweetly by his side, couldn't be happier . . .

From the day I brought the kitten home there was a change in my husband, he didn't go out to the bars nearly as much, he tried to be home every night by dark, and he stoked the fires in both stoves and fussed all over that kitten, somehow he became that kitten's surrogate mother, and not only did my husband meticulously brush his teeth every night, he quit drinking beer at night altogether so as not to reek of it. And whenever I woke up to have a look, there was that kitten suckling at my husband's knuckle, and that's how they slept together, that's how they slept together even when that kitten grew into a full-grown tabby cat, that tabby cat couldn't fall asleep unless he was snuggled up to my husband and suckling at his knuckle. Little Ethan, that's what we named our tabby, was so in love with my husband that he just couldn't wait for evening to come, and when I made the beds Ethan liked to slip under the covers and romp around in the dark, even I fell in love with that tabby, even I fell in love with him as if he were our own little child, even I couldn't wait to see our tabby cat, who was fond of sunning himself up on the roof, up there where my husband typed on his typewriter, in fact, these days my husband even wrote while I was at home, because that tabby cat sat right next to him, gazing wisely at the typewriter keys, gazing love-struck at my husband, and into my lap he would come, and then back to my husband at the typewriter, some sort of muse to my husband is what that little creature was. And so it happened one day that our tabby didn't come home, all night long he didn't come home, my husband was miserable, he went out and poked around the sheds and outbuildings, and the next day he went around to all the neighbors asking if they hadn't seen that little tabby of his. And that jewel of mine combed through every single unoccupied building on that street of ours, calling out and listening for any reply, and he got more miserable by the minute, he was convinced he could hear little Ethan somewhere meowing, but that little tabby cat didn't return all that evening or that night . . . And then in the morning, my husband sat up in bed, and I sat up too . . . and there in the open window perched our tabby cat, one paw poised in the air, seemingly perplexed, as if to say, is anyone home, and am I in the right house, and my husband called to him, and our tabby cat hopped down into the kitchen and set to his milk hungrily, but every so often he stopped wolfing his milk and looked up at my husband and me, as if to say, thank you, and then he went back to his milk, and then he paused and looked up at us again, and both of us knew that without us he would never survive, that someone would surely kill him, and so my husband and I gave each other that same sort of look, the look that said we belonged together, and then a spontaneous kiss to seal how precious we were to one another . . . and our tabby knew it, first he sat in my husband's lap, and then, so there was enough to go around, he came to sit in mine and to gaze into my eyes, and then he gave me a little head butt and shut his eyes, and I, who had never had a cat at home, recognized what it meant to be fond of a little creature, what it meant, as I felt that beautiful strength emanating from his little head, to love him, and I couldn't help myself, I too closed my eyes and gave him a little head butt, and thus we whispered sweet nothings to each other, and my husband and I were happy, as happy as we'd been back in the early days of our romance, when I used to bring my fiancé those little potfuls from the Hotel Paris, when I used to slip him a fifty crown note out of my tips after each shift . . .

Nights, when I was at work and my husband was loafing around the bars, Ethan liked to keep an eye out for us from behind the chimney of that building of ours at number 24 Na Hrázi Street, from his look-out there he could see all the way down to the turn in the street, from where I or my husband would emerge into the glow of the gas lamps, and some nights it was the both of us when my husband came to meet me at the tram. And our tabby sat there on the roof behind the chimney and whenever someone came round that turn in the street out popped his little head and there were those eyes of his locked onto the street, and when I came home alone, or even with that jewel of mine, as soon as I rounded the turn I looked up toward that dimly lit chimney of ours in anticipation of that beloved tabby cat, who disappeared the instant he caught sight of the people he'd been waiting for so patiently, and the minute we unlocked the door from the street there he was on the other side meowing away, and when we opened the door he always stepped out and performed the same ritual, first he brushed up against our legs and then he stretched out a hind leg and then a foreleg and then he switched over and did it again, and I or my husband kneeled down, and our little tabby closed his eyes and stood on his hind legs, for he knew one of us would take him gently under the shoulders and lift him up to cradle him, to press him to our cheek, and just then it was like the fuses fell out of our little tabby, like he fainted, and then he pressed himself to us, and that was exactly the moment we most looked forward to.

So while I kept expecting my husband to return to work, to begin living like a decent person, that jewel of mine kept publishing books, three in a row in fact, and for each one he received an award from the publisher, and whether they published fifty thousand copies, or one hundred thousand, without fail those books were sold out the day after their release . . . All my husband's readers seemed to be a little bit ahead of him, as if they were in a race . . . They consumed those garbled texts of his like they were primers, and my husband kept upping the ante, not just for sheer audacity, but he said things in his texts that shouldn't be said in public, he himself was terrified of that battle he was engaged in with his readers, as if waiting for the gavel to fall, for some judge to pass judgment on those misdemeanors of his, on that hack writing. This gave me a certain amount of pleasure, but the more outrageous my husband was in those texts—and I was convinced that any day now they'd have to shut him down—the more he managed to slip the noose, and in fact he garnered even more awards, in fact those books of his were even published abroad . . .

At work I came across an ad in the *People's Democracy* . . . Will sell a cottage in Kersko. Price: 40,000.00 crowns. I pictured a cottage in the forest, my husband would go out on weekdays, I'd join him for the weekends, and if my husband finds writing difficult now, then how in the world is he going to write once he has a cottage, it'll be doubly hard, and whatever he's working on now will be the last of it, my husband won't have a single solitary reason to write, because he'll have me and his tabby cat and his cottage too, and I knew if we get the cottage that jewel of mine will want to make a fire in every room, in every stove, and where there's no stove he'll put in a new one, and where there's no stovepipe he'll put in a new one, and he'll go from room to room and stoke those stoves, and he'll wander the forests, and I knew just what will happen . . . my husband can't pass by a beautiful birch tree or a beautiful spruce without just standing there, thunderstruck, watching . . . I'll have to be careful he doesn't merge with those trees body and soul, careful not to lose him altogether. And so we answered the advertisement and waited.

And then we received a reply, and put down a deposit on the cottage in Kersko, and then we went out to have a look, and then it was off to the notary to sign the contracts and pay the balance . . . My husband was beside himself with excitement from that forest parcel. He just couldn't wait for everything to be official, for the keys to be his . . . He rode the bus out to visit his forest parcel, to wander around, to ford the little stream . . . he liked to watch those spruce and birch trees, those hundred-and-thirty-year-old trees that would be his, he wasn't so much interested in the building as he was in the spruce and birch, the neighbors of that forest parcel of ours got a little nervous when they saw a stranger lurking, they even went after him, and although he tried to explain the situation, they insisted he remove himself or they'd call police, there were enough shady characters around as it was already. And meanwhile we got our driver's licenses and bought ourselves an Octavia, and then the owners signed back the contracts and gave us the keys and then that parcel and that little kitchen and that little room were ours. And just like I said, my husband's first order of business was to bring in a mason, to cut a second opening into the chimney, and he hooked up a Musgrave stove, and from then on, even when it was hot outside, he always had two stoves going, one in the kitchen and the Musgrave in the living room, those rooms tended to be a little damp there in the forest . . . and as soon as we were settled in my husband started making plans to build a second floor, to raise the roof and build a sort of angled atelier, and he'd put a tin roof on so as to hear the patter of the rain when it came down, just like way back when at the brewery. Those days, when he was into his building plans and his birch trees and his spruce trees, when he wandered the countryside far and wide, he returned from his walks ever more elated, he gave up on his writing altogether, and quit the pubs, he said good-bye to those in-house weddings of his and immersed himself in that countryside he loved so much as a boy, as a young man . . . after all, he used to bring his young ladies here, alongside the river, all the way from Nymburk to the Kersko forests . . .

Mother, I say, please don't take this the wrong way, but I'm more and more certain that that writing of my husband's resembles a *schweinfest.* Mother, if you only heard all the *schweinfest* talk coming from that jewel of mine and the poet Marysko. They just can't wait, they plot and scheme, Mother, they even bought themselves a Slovak handbook for the pig slaughter, *Schweinfests at Home,* it's called, they bought two copies and they study it like it's the Bible. They're raising a piglet at their friends Borek and Milena's place, out in Mléková-Lukosrby, we paid them a visit and Mr. Marysko went to say hello to that piglet of his, but I still wasn't buying it . . . sure enough, once everything was arranged and they'd even invited their friend Waldemar Matuška to the *schweinfest* because he'd attended school in nearby Pátek, they had to put off the pig slaughter thanks to Borek's telegram . . . *Schweinfest on hold. I'm sick. Borek.* And so here we go again, Mother, last week, with my husband and the poet Marysko all primed for the *schweinfest,* we take the train to Mléková-Lukosrby, and because it's so cold out it hurts that jewel of mine buys these bottles of gin and right there on the bus they polish off a whole liter, and, Mother, the whole bus reeks of gin, and when we get off, as we're walking from Chlumec to Lukosrby, there on the main street Mr. Marysko falls back and smacks his head on the cobblestones, and there he lies buried under the three kilos of oranges he's bringing Milena as a gift, and my husband is simply delighted at the sight of his friend lying there buried in oranges . . . I was so ashamed, there on the second floor a window flies open and who should lean out but the local forest ranger in his uniform, he's trying to take a siesta after lunch but the sound of Mr. Marysko's head smacking the cobblestones wakes him up, and he shouts . . . What're you, stupid? And Mr. Marysko comes to his senses, terrified my husband might take a flyer too and shatter those bottles of gin . . . and on we went, Mother, it was just awful . . .

What do you mean awful, says Mother, darling, you're going to have to get used to it, years ago, him and that poet would get so liquored up even I couldn't stand it . . . Down there in that submarine where Mr. Marysko lived, that cellar, they got so blind drunk on gin one time, it was Good Friday, and of course my sonny drank more than anyone else because he wanted to be a writer, an artist, a number one and champion of the world, he drank that gin like it was water . . . And Mr. Marysko had no choice but to load my sonny up on a wagon, and as they wheeled him from the waterworks to the brewery little Karel Marysko rang at each and every house along the way and invited anyone who opened up or leaned out a window to feast their eyes upon my sonny lying there in the wagon, drunk, and thus they brought him to the brewery, and when Grandma opened the door, she didn't see so well anymore, she ran back into the kitchen and clasped her hands . . . They ran over Bora! That was our dog, but luckily it wasn't Bora, it was my sonny . . . We had to call for the doctor because my sonny was unconscious. Darling, there's plenty more in store for you . . .

Mother, I say, you should have seen it, the hugs and kisses and carrying on when we got to Mléková-Lukosrby, no question Milena is in love with the poet Marysko, and they tapped the gin right away and everything was ready and waiting for the slaughter, tubs out in the yard and the winch and chains in the open barn, and freshly baked white bread for the white pudding, and pots full of boiled barley, and no feed for the pig since the night before, and right away the kielbasa was served, and the tinned pork, and they washed it all down with gin, and my husband and Mr. Marysko couldn't be happier, their only regret was that André Breton and Paul Éluard and Tristan Tzara couldn't be there with them, and they laughed it up and Borek drank his beer straight from the bottle, and I was the only one not laughing, I was somewhat apprehensive, in fact, because Borek was a bit of the poet himself, Mother, prone to fabrication, on one occasion we were at Sojka's with a whole bunch of my husband's friends, painters they were, and in walks Borek and says . . . Forgive me, my friends, for being late, but I've just come from my lawyer, you see, for my wife's birthday I've bought her a little something, a villa . . . and everyone was absolutely carried away by this and Borek continued that he required a painter to decorate the manège at the former Kinský manor house in Chlumec, where he raises thoroughbreds, he was prepared to commission those painters to create three six-meter-long canvases as adornment, and he had a budget of two hundred thousand crowns to get it done . . . And get this, Mother, Borek made a deal right then and there with two of the painters, Hample and Bouš . . . But of course, Mother, none of it was true, just like the villa for Milada wasn't true, just like the *schweinfest* to which they'd even invited the likes of Waldemar Matuška wasn't true . . . So, back to Mléková-Lukosrby, we take the lantern and make our way to the cellar, where there's a little stream running through, and Milada's down there transferring marinated meat into a tub, and my husband and the poet Marysko have to get a good whiff of every single piece, even though it stinks to high heaven, and they bring a leg of pork upstairs and Milena makes Wiener schnitzel out of that red meat, and then Doctor Halíř arrives by car and he's sauced to the gills too, but he's just gorgeous, elegant and clean shaven, and this guy, an amateur cellist, is smitten with Mr. Marysko because Marysko is associate concertmaster at the National Theater, and you should have seen it, Mother, the hoopla, the hugs and kisses, especially when Doctor Halíř announced with great fanfare that his mistress gave birth to a baby girl yesterday, that he had to go see her in Hradec Králové . . . Milena told me later it was one of the Doctor's university students fell in love with him, and now he had a beautiful baby girl . . . And Doctor Halíř says he still has to go home tonight because it's his daughter's graduating dance class and they're planning a big to-do and he has to get all dressed up . . . And so I chose to ride with Doctor Halíř into Chlumec that afternoon, so I could make it back, as promised, with the poet Marysko's wife for that famous *schweinfest* in the morning . . . Mother, that car ride with Doctor Halíř was an adventure in and of itself, he was so excited to have a brand new baby girl he drove into the ditch several times, and then, just before we got into the city, he told me he had no intention of going to his daughter's dance class soiree, instead he'd fetch his cello at home and head straight back to Mléková-Lukosrby, he could hardly pass up the chance to hear a still-sober Mr. Marysko play at least part of an Antonín Dvořák concerto on his cello, in honor of tomorrow's *schweinfest,* for the genius composer Dvořák himself had been a trained butcher . . . I relayed all of this, not without a trace of bitterness, to Mother, who got quite a kick out of it, she threw her head back and laughed and said . . . look, darling, I've done my time, now it's your turn to come to terms with it . . . See here, you've got to look at life like it's a slapstick comedy. So what happened next? Mother, I say, when Věra and I got to Mléková-Lukosrby it was afternoon already and the only one left standing was Borek, sucking on a bottle of beer, and Milena was in a rage because of the young butcher . . . I'm gonna kill him! she screamed, waving a huge, greasy knife through the air . . . I'm gonna kill him! He ruined my white pudding, put in half a kilo of ginger, turned it into pastry . . . and there in the middle of the yard was a pile of manure and mired in the muck was a Škoda and passed out behind the wheel with a blissful smile on his face was Doctor Halíř, one arm hanging out the open door buried to the elbow in manure . . . And then, Mother, the strangest procession emerged from the barn, the young butcher with half a pig slung over his shoulder, and next to him walks the poet Marysko, carrying some white pudding, one cheek pressed against the pork leg, enraptured . . . And bringing up the rear is someone so completely plastered it's only by the clothes he wears I recognize that jewel of mine, and he carries a huge pot of raw pork fat, and he's still dressed in those fine new clothes he had tailor-made at Barta on National Avenue, that beautiful shirt and that expensive, now grease-laden necktie, not to mention the perforated dress shoes I brought him back from Vienna, now spattered with manure . . . And Milena called out to us . . . Come and get it, the white and blood pudding are all laid out on the straw . . . Don't stand there like a couple of dopes . . . And so we got our plates and helped ourselves to the goodies, but Miss Věra, the wife of the poet, seemed rather shocked by the goings-on . . . Miss Věra, whose father, as she told me in the car, had been trying for years to obtain the official predicate that would declare him the Baron von Tunkel . . . and now Věra was following in his footsteps because she herself, according to the historical records, was actually the Baroness von Tunkel . . . So, Mother, Miss Věra was quite unsettled there in the kitchen, and she said . . . Milena, what's happening with little Karel? And Milena, in the middle of serving pork barley soup, just waved her off, which made Věra even more nervous . . . Was he really that sick? And Milena downed a shot of gin and said . . . And how, in the morning he lay there in the barn shouting . . . Trocar! And, Mother, through the window I could see my husband in his finest threads slicing pork fat into cubes with a giant knife, he took exquisite care, and looked as focused as when he was writing . . . and suddenly I was overcome with the urge to seize that knife and plunge it into his heart . . . but Miss Věra, who to this day pursues her title of Baroness von Tunkel, kept at Milena . . . Did little Karel puke? And Milena, who had a tic in one eye and a droop to the cheek as a result of stroke, just waved and said with a laugh . . . If only . . . ! And Mr. Marysko walked in, all greasy from having his cheek pressed up to the pork, and said . . . All hail to you, delightful fairies . . . Milena, darling, I'm hungry, get me some of that blood pudding and that barley soup . . . and instead of bread on the side I'll have pig's ear . . . So there you have it, Mother, that slapstick comedy of yours, and then the icing on the cake, in walks Doctor Halíř, fresh off the manure pile, and he stands there with those beautiful eyes of his and says . . . Now the moment has come for Karel, associate concertmaster of the National Theater, to play us a passage of Dvořák on his cello . . .

Mother, when she finished laughing, just waved her hand as if to say that's all peanuts compared to what I'm about to tell you . . . and the more we talked the more I understood why her son was the way he was, why he wouldn't change, why he would stay the same, despite our mutual conviction that we could make him into a decent person . . . but why was he the way he was? Why, when in fact he was a shy and timid person, was he compelled to be number one and champion of the world in eating and drinking, why was he always fleeing from us, and when unable to flee, why the awful theatrics, the showing off? Mother recalled how at every *schweinfest* her sonny had to be number one, had to stuff himself to bursting with the blood pudding, but only when we had guests, when he was showing off . . . when alone all he had was one sausage, sliced into pieces with some bread on the side and a little beer . . . Every autumn, Mother said, the landlord gave us a bounty of partridge, I cooked two roasting pans full, sixteen partridge at a time, and that sonny of mine, if we had guests, showed off by eating four partridge all by himself . . . but when alone, all he had was one little partridge . . . Or smoked meat? I brought back a whole basketful from the smokehouse, and when alone he just nibbled at it, but when we had company he wolfed it down like there was no tomorrow, not even bread on the side, he ate so much of that smoked meat everyone else felt inferior, but the next day he just lay in bed, sick . . . But why does he do it?

Mother, I say, that jewel of mine always acts as if he's just done something wrong, he himself says he always feels like he's just gotten a bad report card and is scared to go home . . . Mother, somewhere in his past something must have happened to him, that's why he's always on the run, and though he likes spending time at home, the minute I arrive he's off again like a shot . . . now that we've bought ourselves the cottage, Mother, I wouldn't mind so much if he absconded to the bars, that would be fine, but the chief of the local SNB police tells me he often spies my husband through his binoculars lying down there in the field in a haystack, and when the chief's back from doing his rounds in the Volha a few hours later, my husband's lying there still, arms splayed and staring at the sky . . . There's tractor tracks leading right up to that haystack, Mother, ending there . . . like a small plane lifted off just as it reached the haystack . . . made for the sky . . . and that's where my jewel lies, buried up to his shoulders in hay . . . that's where he runs to and that's where he finds his peace and reporting it all back to me is the chief of police . . .

Mother grew serious, and then, as if it pained her to remember the past, she began . . . Come to think of it, I often saw him climbing the ladder up to the hayloft, darling, there was enough hay up there for four pair of horses and two pair of oxen, sometimes he spent hours up there . . . And then in the little forest glen, down by the birch trees, he built himself a sort of tin shack, even had a stove inside, a windowless shack, and that's where he holed up, stoking the stove, outside the sun was shining but there was my sonny, crawled into the dark, inside a tin shack you could hardly stand up in . . . As a boy he never liked coming home, and when he was at his university studies, crawling up into the attic was his thing, the attic above our flat, and when it stormed that tin roof up there drummed with the falling rain, and that sonny of mine walled in a corner of the attic for himself, the only corner that had a skylight to the heavens, and often I heard him ascending the stairs . . . in fact, he fled from the brewery to that Libeň flat too . . . and why? Probably because there's never any sun there either, and he has to have the stoves going even in summer, but doubtless the main reason he fled to Libeň was to hole up in there and be alone, he had to arrange and buy everything for himself, had to whitewash the walls on his own . . . But nowadays, what is it that drives him to bury himself up to the shoulders inside that haystack? Darling, now it's dawning on me, what I'm going to tell you is no slapstick anymore, or maybe, in the final analysis, it really is . . . You see, I had that sonny of mine out of wedlock . . . Back then it was something shameful . . . I remember the Sunday I told my parents, Mother was making lunch while I sprang it on Father that I was pregnant and that my boyfriend had no intention of marrying me just yet . . . and my quick-tempered father grabbed me by the shoulder and shoved me down, he dragged me out to the yard and then fetched his hunting rifle and shouted . . . On your knees, I'm gonna shoot you! And I was so scared, I begged him for mercy . . . But my wise mother came outside and said . . . Enough already, come on and eat before it gets cold . . .

It began before dawn, I found that jewel of mine on the floor, at first I thought he was drunk, sometimes he came home completely liquored up while I was still at work, and crawled into bed, and lying there like that you couldn't tell he was all wobbly and barely able to string two words together, on the contrary, he was quite pleasant as he lay there in bed, smiling. But now he writhed around on the floor, pleading for the good Lord to take him away, he claimed to have a pain in his stomach, in his liver, so bad it was like someone cutting him open with a red-hot knife. And as soon as he said it he balled up and writhed around on the floor some more, and he was hit with the urge to throw up and go to the toilet at the same time, and he was ashen and his eyes were more beautiful than I'd ever seen, he begged me to take him by the hand, he promised that from now on he would behave, that he would drink only mineral water, that we would begin our life anew, and again he wanted me to hold his hand and caress him, and he took up Ethan and lay him across his forehead as you would a compress, but Ethan the tabby cat pulled away from my husband, in fact he even put back his ears like a mean horse. And then Ethan crawled under the bed and my husband took that as a sign he was about to die, for a cat had the ability to predict its master's death. And then my husband began to throw up again, he pleaded with me to stay by his side, he moaned and lamented, and I brought him a bucket, and I'm not even sure why, but I was glad he was in the grips of that attack, as if that gallbladder heard my plea, as if that bloated liver was the period or the exclamation point on all my good advice and exhortation, how many times had I begged him not to drink so much, not to eat those smoked pork hocks, not to eat that bacon dredged in pepper, and the more he writhed and moaned, the more I smiled, I swapped out the buckets into which he wailed plaintively, like he was playing the French horn . . . Ethan, when he crawled out from under the bed, his hair on end, sniffed at that bucket of vomit and took off like a shot through the open window, and at my husband's behest I threw open all the windows, he begged for fresh air . . . and so that jewel of mine bid me farewell, bid farewell to Libeň, bid Prague and all his friends farewell . . . it was akin to when he came home drunk, when he drank those ten beers of his, when I was in bed already and he came in with that stupid smile on his face and plunked down on the bed, it's a wonder he never broke my legs, and he sat there with that smile on his face and relayed who all had sent their hellos . . . and Mirda the swordsman sends his hello, and Vladimir says hello, and Vávra senior says hello—he's about to publish with Mladá Fronta—and Mr. Marysko and Mr. Bufil say hello, and a hundred hellos from the waiter at Pinkas, and then the waiter at The Tomcat, and sending you a special hello is the waiter at The Golden Tiger . . . thus he listed off all those people he knew, who sent their hellos out just for me . . . and now as he lay dying on the floor of his flat, lay on the floor moaning and throwing up, now as the cat bolted out the window in a clear signal to its master he was about to die, my husband begged me to relay his greetings, to tell all those friends of his that they were in his thoughts at the very moment he was on the brink . . . and say hello to Mirda the swordsman, and to Vladimir, and say hello to the waiter at Pinkas, and to both waiters at The Two Cats, and to all the surrealists, and say hello to my brother . . . and when he was done listing everyone he knew he seemed to feel better, and he asked me for some paper and a pen and to put it on the floor for him, so that in between his bouts of vomiting and spasms down there on the floor he might compose his last will and testament, which began with the words . . . In the event the Lord summons me to the great beyond, I hereby order . . . and he bequeathed all his possessions to me, and to his friends his books, and our cottage there at number 248 in Kersko he bequeathed to the Polaban Semice football club, so they might have some place to gather before a match, like the Dukla club had Vonoklasy . . . I paced back and forth, I stood in the open doorway and watched the amber light of dawn come over the rooftops . . . that was another of my husband's little habits, if we flew let's say to Brno, my husband left his last will on the kitchen table, and the same thing when he took those trips of his abroad, from where he never brought me back anything, except for a pair of glasses once, but those he picked up at the Prague station, although he claimed they were special glasses, all the way from London . . . anyway, those last wills of his were almost always of a piece, if we traveled somewhere by car or bus he bequeathed everything to me, and by airplane he bequeathed everything to his brother, and his books to his friends and the cottage in Kersko to the Polaban Semice football club . . . From the moment my husband became a famous writer he feared for his life, even out on the street he stuck strictly to the curb, always looking up, he would have walked in the middle of the street if not for traffic, for he was convinced that all the moldings on all the buildings were just waiting to steal his life away, to feast upon the fact they'd snuffed out such a famous and beautiful writer . . . And next door to our flat was that lab and machine shop, and the morning shift was just coming on, and like every day, those giant saws and lathes would cut through axles and steel frames in order to gauge their strength, and every ten minutes or so something behind that wall directly adjacent to our kitchen would rumble to the floor with such force the foundation shuddered, and every few hours a shot so thunderous would ring out it would send the plaster tearing away, the plaster the masons from the machine shop reapplied once a month . . . and when that first huge shot of the day rang out, when somewhere in the depths of that machine shop a severed axle crashed to the ground, that's exactly when my husband completed his last will and testament and was released from the grips of that gallbladder attack . . . He got up, and absolutely broken, shuffled off to bed and lay down, I emptied the bucket of throw up, got him some fresh water and bathed him with a wet cloth, I sponged down his chest, and then I called Ethan over, I petted him and picked him up, I stood there with him in the open door for a while, and as usual Ethan pretended to have fainted in my arms, and we whispered sweet nothings to each other, and then I carried him over to the bed, where my husband lay all cleaned up, eyes closed, he looked like a corpse just then, and I put Ethan on the bed, and my husband reached out to pet him and Ethan gave his hand a little head butt and meowed, and then he curled up onto the pillow beside my husband's head and suckled at his knuckle and fell sweetly asleep . . . And my husband opened his eyes and smiled at me, and although I frowned back, I knew that jewel of mine had the worst of it behind him . . .

And we had an in-house wedding in that building of ours, Jenda from the flat upstairs was getting married, the guy who always tried to avoid me and when he couldn't flushed red . . . but taking my husband as an example he began to drink, and he talked himself up a pretty girl, she was that sort of Viennese bowling pin type, and when he got drunk he was wont to yell at her, I hardly even recognized him, and they mailed out the wedding announcements and got married at the Little Chateau on Šlosberk, same as I, and then the wedding reception at Cafeteria World, and after the reception the guests came over to Jenda's place to toast the newlyweds, and late that afternoon, when everyone was gone, Jenda staggered downstairs in his wedding clothes and his myrtle and his crazy smile, and Ethan the cat flew out the window, terrified of the drunken Jenda, who carried a bottle of vodka in one hand and a shot glass in the other, and Jenda plunked himself down, drenched in sweat from the alcohol, and then he poured my husband a shot and put it in front of him . . . Mr. Hrabal, I am your student, you showed me the way, reading your books made me into a human being again, I'm not afraid of anyone anymore, drink a toast to me . . . ! And my husband looked like he was going to throw up, like he'd taken the cure at Professor Skála's, been given the Antabuse . . . and throw up he did, and then he patted Jenda on the back and led him outside, congratulated him, bowed to him, and then Jenda started up the steps but he collapsed there on the fourth one and fell asleep, fell fast asleep in his wedding clothes, I saw the bride all dressed in white dragging Jenda up step by step, she was a formidable bride, the bowling pin Viennese type, and once she got him upstairs and into bed . . . there was no one in the yard, no one looking through the windows opposite, and leaning over the balcony railing she threw her veil in the air, it was a beautiful sight to see, that young bride standing there surrounded by our crumbling building, a picture perfect bride straight out of a magazine, and I watched her and gave her a smile . . .

In the end I was happy my husband brought back that huge, three-meter-long mirror from Piešťany and hung it on our wall, as soon as I walked into our little courtyard, if our windows were open, I saw my reflection, bathed in sunshine, then immersed in shadow, I saw myself reflected in that mirror on the wall, and then I was gone, and when I entered our flat, even if the sun was shining outside I had to turn on all the lights, that's how cold and deep the shade was . . . When my husband wasn't at home, I liked to prance around before this mirror, sometimes I stood here and examined myself closely, this mirror had been with me ever since I was little, I looked into it as a young girl, and then as a young woman, and finally, before they loaded us up and shipped us off to a holding camp, I looked into it to see my father going away . . . And when we started life anew there in Piešťany, this mirror reflected not just my life, but Papa's, and my little brother

Heini's . . . and we were all so looking forward to going to Germany on our collective passport, but the only ones to get a permit were Mother and Papa . . . and Heini and I, because we'd gone to Czech schools, had to stay put . . . it was in this mirror I saw Papa preparing to leave for the station, saw him going away . . . and then we stood on the platform . . . and then the train . . . and then the tears . . . and then we came back home and forevermore it was just me and Heini in this mirror . . . and then one last time I saw myself in this mirror in Piešťany, it was when I no longer wanted to live, when everything in the world was unbearable, I looked into this very mirror and saw in my eyes that I couldn't stay in this world any longer, that I couldn't live, I saw a woman who'd lost at love, lost that jewel of hers . . . and so I looked at myself in this mirror and swallowed two handfuls of pills, I looked at myself and saw my reflection begin to blur, and before I passed out, I suddenly saw my whole life flash before me in this mirror . . .

I'll often stop and take a good look at myself, here, in Libeň, on the verge of immortality, as my husband likes to say . . . ever since he's published several novels, he really does feel he's on the verge of immortality, but I do too, here in this mirror I see myself from the other side somehow, but I have to be alone before this mirror, never with my husband around, and often I see myself, how downtrodden I was back when I lived at Jirka's mother's place, Jirka, whom I'd already forgotten, forgotten that guitar of his, and even those Spanish guitar solos he used to play me . . . but when that single solitary letter from my Auntie Pišinka in Vienna arrived there in Žižkov, it opened my eyes and shamed me to the core . . . And from the moment I received that letter I began to look after myself, I bought those red high heels and new clothes and lingerie, on account of what Auntie wrote me from Vienna . . . if you don't want people to treat you as slop, you must try to display yourself as a pastry from *Paris* . . . And indeed now I am that pastry from *Paris,* every day I examine myself in the mirror, so that when I go out, I am ready for the world . . . I practically sniff at myself in this mirror, as I put on my eye shadow and my eyeliner . . . And half a year after I visited Karli in Vienna he wrote to inform me that Auntie Pišinka, who knew just how to display herself as a pastry from *Paris,* had had a frilly new nylon ball gown made . . . and on Christmas Eve, as she was running over to the Christmas tree to express her admiration, she brushed past the blazing fireplace, and the ball gown burst into flames . . . that frilly *Parisien* nylon ball gown . . . even the fluttering nylon scarf caught fire . . . as did her wig . . . And these days Auntie Pišinka often walks with me through this cold flat of mine, and when I look myself over in the mirror, I often see Auntie's face leaning out behind me, Auntie, whom I last saw when I was a little girl . . . but now here in Libeň, from the other side so to speak, I often see her leaning out behind me, and whispering in my ear . . . you must always display yourself and be as *appetitlich* as a pastry from *Paris* . . .

That jewel of mine liked looking at himself in the mirror, but he never sat down to do it, he just paced around, stopped to get a load of himself, then paced some more, lost in thought . . . often I saw him as I came home from work, I saw the flat from the courtyard, lights blazing, the lamp and the furniture reflected in the mirror. When the in-house weddings used to go on here, from the courtyard it always looked like the flat was overflowing with people, but that was because the whole wedding party was reflected over and over again. My husband had a peculiar way of looking at himself in the mirror. He examined his face to see how he had aged, he looked at his eyes, he put his hands on the mirror and leaned in and eyed himself closely, he could never get his fill . . . And I knew this was the way someone looks at themselves, examines themselves, when they know they're very sick, when they know they might be dead inside of a year, that's how my jewel looked at himself, and when the gallbladder trouble let up, he refused to believe it, he scrutinized himself in the mirror, his condition, and often he pulled down his eyelids to check for jaundice, he felt the lines around his mouth, those sunken cheeks of his, felt the bags under his eyes, and he was never happy with what he saw there in the mirror, quite the contrary, he grew more and more somber, scared even, but it wasn't just what happened to him that scared him, it was what happened to everyone else too, the thing is, my husband considered what happened to other people the same as if it happened to him . . .

This time after the attack he could only sip at his Pilsner beer, and he wasn't allowed even a bite of fatty pork meat—and my husband loved his pork belly and his roast pork hock—boiled beef was all he got now, and he walked slower than he used to, it was me in the lead for a change, and I relished running up ahead and turning back and shouting, What's taking you so long? But actually I wasn't happy about it, quite the contrary, it made me angry because I could see there was nothing wrong with him anymore, but that gallbladder put such a scare into my husband that he was shocked to still be alive and kicking, he, who was fond of dishing out advice to the seriously ill, was now terrified, constantly probing at his stomach, when in fact there was nothing wrong with him . . . he scrutinized himself, he liked to visit Doctor Adam to inquire about his blood test, but Doctor Adam just laughed and waved his hand, he told my husband there was nothing wrong with him, that he still had plenty of time, that neither he nor his blood showed any sign of cancer or cirrhosis of the liver, he was, however, a prime candidate—like everyone in the same boat—for one heck of a gallstone, which, when the time came, would be removed . . . But that jewel of mine, when he came home from seeing Doctor Adam, sat before the mirror and claimed the doctor was hiding something, that he could see it in his eyes, that he didn't want to give it to him straight, and that he and the nurse were whispering behind his back, and when my husband turned to look, Doctor Adam simply clammed up . . .

And so this man, who meted out optimism wherever he went, who walked the streets of the city like a lighted torch and stormed the pubs with Vladimir, always tipsy and full of laughter, this same man now went about as if scalded, he gawked and was skittish of everyone and everything, unsure of himself, as if he'd done something wrong . . . and I strode along ahead of him, I was at the top of my game those days, I wore the greatest outfits, and even if it was nice out, carried my little parasol . . . once, when my husband and Vladimir were on a bender, he bought me two silk parasols, one blue and one pink, but in fact he bought those parasols more for himself than for me, given that every time he emerged from a pub to see something in a store window he liked he went straight in and bought it, one time it was a winter cap, he bought four of them, expensive, woolen winter caps, another time he brought home two Scottish scarves, he never wore scarves of course, he claimed he always had to wear his shirt open at the neck . . . and so on that occasion they came home with two parasols, one pink and one blue, and the sun was shining, and into the courtyard came those two parasols, gifts from my husband and Vladimir . . . but the two of them covered most of Prague with those parasols before coming home, they dropped into their pubs and were thrilled to be the center of attention, because sporting those parasols they were number ones and champions of the world . . . And I bought two pairs of the same shoes, red high heels, Italian, and I stepped out in those shoes, while my husband toddled along behind me like a lame dog, turning, looking over his shoulder, an awfully sad expression in his eyes, and he told me with a whisper that just then he passed by Death's door, that he saw Death watching him, that of course in the past he'd read about this sort of thing, but now that he was so chronically, almost mortally ill, he saw it for real, Death, watching him from afar through a pair of binoculars, laughing . . .

. . . Then there was the time he went out alone to Brno-Židenice, to visit the grave of his grandmother and grandfather, and the grave of his Uncle Bob, to spend two days at the old family house on Balbínova, where his cousin Jirka now lived, who had the same catlike face as my husband, the high cheekbones, descended, as my husband liked to boast, from Avars and Tatars . . . and my husband arrived at the old house below the Židenice cemetery and climbed the narrow circular staircase to the attic, where Jirka had stored all the old furniture he didn't particularly fancy, the furniture my husband grew up in, the bed he was born in, and the paintings of saints, now turned to face the attic wall . . . and everything was neatly stored and waiting for some relative to come take it all away . . . And there in the attic my husband arranged the furniture as it once was, he sat down at the little table with the plush red cover, upon which lay the plush photo album filled with photographs of his forbears, whole teams of men and women with those high cheekbones, beautiful women and stern-looking men, life had left its mark on those families . . . and up there in the attic my husband ran a hand over everything, he looked at those saints again, those paintings he'd looked at when he was a child, the first paintings he ever saw, lying in his baby carriage . . . there in the attic he even hung the old swag lamp that once ran on oil . . . and when he said good-bye to all of that my husband came home, and he brought back a spice rack, a sort of small cupboard with little drawers, and each drawer was adorned with an enamel plaque . . . Ginger . . . Pepper . . . Allspice . . . and Vanilla had its own special little drawer . . . He brought along the spice rack and swore to me that this was only a minute representation of all the beautiful things, of all the beautiful furniture, that lay in that attic, furniture he'd lived in as a wee babe, as a three-year-old boy, and then during every single holiday, it was a must we bring back that kitchen and living room furniture, in fact we would move, buy a new flat, so as to accommodate that living room and that kitchen exactly as they were when he first laid eyes on the world.

. . . And so that jewel of mine, when he was feeling good, loved to tell the story of how he almost drowned in Polná, he went on with great zeal, just so people would admire him, so they would arrive at the same conclusion he had, that he was king of the world, number one, champion of the republic, even when it came to something as banal as drowning, and on his way back from Židenice he stopped off in Polná to visit the brewery, to hearken back to the time when as a three-year-old boy he sat there in the kitchen and the whole world went spinning around him because he was so drunk he couldn't even untie his shoelaces, and there was the old gate to the street, which buzzed with students from the nearby grammar school and junior high, and there was the confectioner's house, Mr. Hazuka . . . but mainly he wanted to visit and pay his respects to the little stream he fell into way back when, he swallowed so much water the rumor went around town he drowned, and the local kids stopped by to offer up little pictures of saints for his coffin . . . so my husband sat by the stream, in order to relish his first brush with death, death by tragic circumstance, he sat there feeling sorry for himself, sorry that Death was coming for him now, in Libeň, and like every death, was coming when least convenient . . . And then he spent the whole afternoon in the Polná town square, feeling the warm fountain sandstone heated by the sun off the water, the water he almost drowned in when he was five years old . . . it was a Sunday morning, and a woman spied him through her window, the thing is, she'd suffered a gallbladder attack, so while everyone else was at their Sunday lunch she sat alone, and thus saw the boy fall into the fountain. And so my husband retraced his birth, retraced his drowning and his resurrection, which he owed to Doctor Michálek, the same gentleman who had examined Anežka Hrůzová when she was found in the Březina forest with her throat slit . . . so said my husband with a laugh whenever he told anyone about those deaths of his.

Then there was the time that jewel of mine and I set off for Nymburk, the place he'd spent the best years of his life, those years that forever nurtured in him the sense that he belonged to that River Labe country. He led me only through those streets, and only to those structures, that had remained unchanged from his boyhood . . . I had to walk the narrow streets with him past the stinking embankments, I had to lean back and gaze up at the water tower, the art nouveau water tower capped off with a gigantic grill, a sort of royal crown made of steel, which for the moment was removed and lay on the ground beside the tower. I had to feel the stone parapet of the bridge, the structure of the stone, because he used to run his fingers along this particular parapet on his way home from school. I had to go into the church of Saint Giles with him, he showed me where he used to stand as a schoolboy, because catechist Nikl handed out gold stars to those who attended church on Sunday, and, as my husband claimed, he enjoyed going to church . . . Then my husband showed me a stone wall and railing on Jízdecká Street, the same wall a bunch of schoolboys once stood under in anticipation of a miracle by the poet Marysko, who promised them that even though it was sunny out he could conjure up the rain, because he, the poet, was a magician too . . . He ordered the kids to stand there and close their eyes, and then the poet himself climbed upon the wall and peed on the kids below . . . In Nymburk my husband and I stood before a renaissance gate, which led to the executioner's house, and then we stood before the huge gate of the rectory, the gate that would forever remain shut, my husband and I peered through a chink in the gate and all that was left were a few statues, a dilapidated garden fence, a fallen monument, and a giant, red tower. I looked into the deacon's garden, and I saw how excited my husband was to show me everything, and how interested he was in my reaction. And I didn't consider any of those buildings, any of that famous bygone era, particularly noteworthy . . . I strolled on with my little parasol, however, and expressed my amazement . . . Really? Is it possible? Who would have thought . . . And he even led me to the brewery, I must admit I was curious to see how his mother and father had lived, their heart had always been at the brewery, for they spent their happiest years here, just as I had spent my happiest years in Hodonín, at least until the end of the war . . . But the foreman's flat where his parents once lived looked good only from afar . . . There were different kinds of people living here now, with different ways, it looked like they were squatting here, next to the front door was a makeshift pigsty, and when we looked into the courtyard even my husband seemed to wilt, there were so many tools and so much junk and rusted machinery about . . . and those famous rooftops my husband wanted to show me—from where he used to gaze out at the countryside, the rooftops four stories high above the coolers and barley stores—he no longer dared, because everything in that famous brewery of his had changed . . . I'm here for the last time, he said to the brewery, and on our way back to town my husband was quiet, and then, like he'd just come out of a dream, he looked around, and leaned over the parapet of the bridge, he gazed at the mud-covered banks, and at the water's surface, beneath which flowed the river of his childhood, a different river altogether, a brown river the color of alder sap . . . And suddenly, as I reached the far side of the bridge, my husband strode past me in that characteristic way of his, casting about with that rude smirk on his face . . . he was fond of telling me that back when he was a boy, if some guy caught him with that smirk on his face, he climbed down off his bike and gave him a good slap, and then, satisfied he righted something in the universe gone awry, he climbed back up on his bike and rode away . . .

My husband liked to describe himself as having the type of character that changed several times a day, he said that for a few hours he'd have a smile on his face, feeling as fine as if he'd just won the lottery, and then a few hours later it was like he was sniffing a turd . . . he said his character was akin to April weather, that he had a bit of the manic depressive in him, a few hours of high-spirited perspective dished out to himself and anyone within earshot, followed for the rest of the day by thoughts of slipping into the void. So that's the way it was, this he claimed was his character, but when it came to me, I had to be in a perpetual good mood, as soon as he saw that I was in the doldrums, that my mood too could swing like April weather, he immediately began to lecture me on how to restore my equilibrium, and he read to me from Seneca on spiritual peace, for he absolutely could not tolerate for me to be down, not even for a while.

Only later did I begin to understand it . . . When I came home I spied him from the courtyard sitting on a chair examining himself in the mirror, no doubt he'd been sitting there for at least an hour, I saw him looking into the mirror, trying to make sense of who he was, it was akin to the urge he had to revisit his past, revisit Nymburk, and from Nymburk Polná, and from Polná all the way back to Židenice, to where he was born . . . he was perpetually trying to level some charge against himself, that was something I really valued about my husband, he really did think the worst of himself, he searched his past for precisely those events he feared most, those events he'd sealed up like a broken window in a dilapidated building, like a poisoned well. Perhaps that's why he turned to his feminine side for respite, that's why he liked flowers, why he liked to arrange bouquets, from the first snowdrops to autumn crocus, he loved to stroll for hours on end, to wander the Kersko forests and meadows, always to return with flowers. My husband had these stubby fingers, bruised and battered and stiff from his spade work in Kladno, but when it came to picking flowers, he got this dopey look on his face, he only picked those wildflowers that grew off on their own somewhere, he didn't like store-bought flowers, in fact never bought them . . . because picking those first snowdrops, still there under the snow, was a celebration for my husband, like going to confirmation, and I wasn't allowed to talk to him, wasn't allowed to look at him, he couldn't stand me looking at him when he was engaged in something beautiful, he always wanted to be at it alone, which was a good thing, because I was never into picking flowers myself, I had no relationship to flowers, all the flowers I ever had at home refused to bloom, as if on purpose . . . while clivia thrived in other people's windows, that eager spray of red flowers never blossomed in mine, a flower that had no trouble blooming elsewhere on my watch never bloomed, not even a Jericho rose, not even a passion flower bloomed under my care, and those flowers were like me, they shared my fate, my husband intimated as much to me, he was concerned as to why we hadn't any children, as to why not a single plant flowered in our home, and he'd ask me—and I'd tell him where he could go with such questions—if I wasn't hiding a kid somewhere, because perhaps we could take him back, and maybe our home wouldn't be exactly happy, but at least it would be a step up from where it was now.

My husband brought home handfuls of snowflakes and primrose and lily of the valley, he returned from his walks through the forest scented with fresh air, he carried those flowers proudly, like he carried Ethan the cat around that forest parcel of ours, our miserable and skittish cat, who hated the forest and meadows, who much preferred our courtyard in Libeň, the rooftops and the sheds and the dust . . . my husband carried our cat around proudly, like those flowers of his, he showed him all the new leaves on the bushes, the various plants, he wandered the property and held Ethan in his arms and described to him what everything was called, he even had him sniff at things, or touch some low-hanging tree branch with a paw . . . When the birch and larch trees began to green, my husband made his flower bouquets by mixing in a few sprigs of periwinkle and a couple of birch and larch branches, and then he bound it all together with a plain old hemp rope . . . That's how he made his bouquets, which he then distributed, always one to me and the rest to the pretty women in Kersko, those young women who came for the weekend just like us, just like the other cottage owners and their friends . . . And when he handed out those bouquets it always made him think of his grandmother, Kateřina, Katyna, Kati, who'd had the most beautiful garden back in Židenice, filled with such an array of flowers she could make bouquets virtually the year round, from lily of the valley to aster to straw flower, his grandmother had a sacramental relationship to flowers, she most loved the flowers that reflected her faith, she loved Christ and the Virgin Mary like they were her own family, like they had never died and were eternally young, and grandmother's favorite flower, as my husband said with feeling, was the bleeding heart, with its heart-shaped flowers, and forget-me-nots, and peonies on the Feast of Corpus Christi, and then the beloved white lily Saint Anthony had so loved to hold.

. . . My husband loved and was fascinated by crocuses, in spring he showed me the dark green leaves sprouting in the first meadows, he said those crocus leaves would wither, but come fall, after the hay was cleared, they would blossom with purple flowers, which my husband would pick and carry home carefully, he never made a bouquet of them, but arranged them in a glass of water instead, and those crocuses lasted practically the whole month through, those purple flowers with the transparent, almost crystalline stems . . . When lilac was in bloom, kids descended on it and tore off whole branches, my husband made bouquets from what was left over, and the kids set to the pussy willows as well when they were in bloom, and using his scissors my husband clipped whatever was left over and arranged the branches into a pot or a tub or a beer stein . . . but my husband never liked ornamental lilac, he preferred wild lilac, the sort that grew out in the country cemeteries, in the abandoned farmhouse gardens and courtyards, that was his lilac, blue lilac, like blue eyes welling with tears, his raven-haired Aunt Černošková had those eyes, light blue eyes as blue as a forget-me-not . . . Whenever my husband brought home lilac, I knew he'd say . . . That's the color of my eyes, I had eyes like that, when I was young . . . To which I never said anything, I always pretended not to hear, and looked out into the yard like something out there utterly fascinated me . . .

My husband and his writing, that was an awfully confusing mess, he didn't even care about the style of the writing, didn't even try . . . I was no expert in grammar, but I was quite certain my husband didn't know how to write Czech correctly, his writing seemed to me like a translation from a foreign language, simply notes waiting to be expanded upon, simply scratching the surface of events that required more diligent work . . . But that's precisely what my husband was proud of, he was keen on leaving those texts of his unfinished, in half ruin, with the plaster fallen away and the crumbling brick wall beneath it laid bare . . . My husband and that writing of his were rather like those Prague courtyards, with their sections of scaffolding scattered about, and their overflowing trash cans, that writing of my husband's was the forgotten and discarded remains of old material, spare parts, wiring, ducts, all the junk that got carted away on scrap metal Sundays . . . my husband's writing seemed a reflection of all that . . . he said those yards around Harfa were an embodiment of his texts, the broken windows of the incinerator plant, the busted glass of the ČKD factory, he said you could even draw a line between his writing and the way the workers dressed. He liked going to Harfa for lunch, to the Bratislava restaurant, and sitting there . . . it was all bygone, he told me, those Monday mornings when every worker brought along a freshly laundered pair of overalls, so clean they shone, nowadays they wore their overalls until they came apart at the seams, used wire to mend the holes, and some of the workers even went to lunch in those Vysočany pubs in overalls so tattered and scrapped they looked like clowns, my husband told me it was in fashion, the way they dressed, just like pissoirs and bathrooms so dirty they even made my husband shudder were in fashion . . . made him shudder, yes, horrified him, yes, but the minute he had some free time he was off to Harfa, to drop in on those two pubs of his, to wander past those factories and yards, and he just had to be alone, because it focused and enchanted him, all that devastation and ruin, even those outfits the workers wore, but those same workers, when the siren blew, when it was time to punch out, when the shift was over, emerged from those shops and factories freshly bathed and squeaky clean, like someone waved a magic wand, well-dressed people they were, in jeans and brightly colored jackets, and they crowded into those same pubs and drank their beer and laughed and carried on . . . My husband claimed that the most bedraggled workers in Libeň and Vysočany actually had the nicest flats, with wall-to-wall carpeting, those same workers, when they came home, removed their shoes in the foyer, not only did they have beautiful kitchens, but dining rooms as well, in fact even their children had their own rooms, and my husband said these workers loved to dress well, they had slick bathrooms and fancy WCs, but as soon as it was time to go back to work in those Vysočany and Libeň shops and factories, out came the dirty, tattered work clothes, and not even the stinking pissoirs and the paper-clogged toilets seemed to bother them . . .

From everything Mother told me about my husband, and even from what he told me about himself, I formed a strange picture of him, the thing is, he was extremely susceptible to his surroundings, so as the times changed so too did my husband, he even saw this as a virtue, as an asset, a reflection of not just his style of living, but his style of writing as well . . . Those first texts he wrote are the only ones I like, poems delicate, gentle and shy, Mother told me he wrote them when he was in love with Georgine, a sixteen-year-old girl, daughter of a state factory worker who owned a little house in Zálabí . . . and it was first love, Mother said, a first love so fragile that after four years it fell apart, because that Georgine was so beautiful it literally made my son ill, he couldn't handle beauty, beautiful girls scared him, as soon as he saw a beautiful woman he grew skittish, feverish, it only took fifteen minutes for Georgine to send him into a fever, he blushed and stuttered, could think of nothing but Georgine, even the doctor had to stop by to check on him for he couldn't get a wink of sleep, how he could have studied law I have no idea, Mother said, at noon he was already on his way back from Prague and it was straight to Georgine and the afternoon walks along the River Labe, that river sure let him have it . . . I hoped he'd mingle with other people too when he was with Georgine, but those Sunday afternoons on the promenade in town were more than enough for my son, first thing in the morning he was up ironing his pants, polishing his shoes, he even put shoe cream on the soles of his shoes, then he took forever to shave, and from all his tossing and turning at night his hair was a mess, so he had to douse it with oil and comb it out with a brush, and then he had to wear a hairnet for an hour, or he had this black cap with a string you tied under your chin, like swimmers had back then, and after that it took him forever to select a shirt and necktie, he must have gone through a dozen shirts and neckties, and he always had beautiful clothes, suits tailor made in Prague, and he also had kid gloves and a gray hat from Čekan's in Prague, the most beautiful gray hat with a black band, but I wasn't allowed to look at him, if I did he yelled at me, it was obvious how my son feared that promenade, sure he went, but it was like he was afraid of himself, like he felt he wasn't good enough for Georgine, that girl from the outskirts of town whose outfits were just thrown together . . . On his return from the promenade he'd take off his jacket and his shirt was soaked with sweat, even when it was cool in spring, even when it was cold in fall, he stripped down and cooled his head under the wide open faucet for the longest time . . .

. . . So somehow he repeated that love of mine, Mother said, I fell in love too, my first love, it was my everything, the way it should be with first love, but I was pregnant, too, and all these unfamiliar things were happening to me, I was in shock and scared by that pregnancy, by that first love, I was dying of fear, I didn't want to live anymore because of that first love and that child inside of me, I was dying of shame, until, as you've already heard, I told them at home and my father wanted to shoot me but my mother just said . . . Come on and eat, or your Sunday lunch will get cold . . . And so that first love of mine abandoned me and I was ashamed and frightened, back in the Austrian Empire it was shameful to have a child out of wedlock, and that child in fact shared my own fate, that child inherited the same fear of love, the dread, the humiliation which I could not escape myself . . . that first love of mine, that transgression, essentially haunts me my entire life, it's why my son was so devastated by his own first love, he locked himself in his room and typed up those first verses of his, only then he found a little peace, but those verses were just like his love for Georgine, he was ashamed of them, he blushed whenever he showed them to anyone, same as he did whenever he introduced Georgine or brought her around to our place, and after four years of going out with Georgine he was still ashamed, not of her, but of his love for her, a type of love that he inherited from me . . . a love like that is a wonderful thing, but a sin as well . . . Back then he took great pains with the way he looked, he loved to dress up, but because of Georgine he kept upping the ante, doing everything to look better and better, nicer shoes and nicer neckties, all for Georgine, but inevitably he was disappointed with the way he looked, he always wanted to be someone else, someone he could never be, someone like Konečný, the teacher, or like the young actors who used to call on me, handsome men with impeccable manners and social graces, men who knew the art of conversation, men who could just sit there with a cigarette and look good, and all this combined just drove my son to ruin, he flushed red, unable to string a sentence together, and if so, it was completely off topic, he crawled away to his room, there to give himself hell, to swear at himself in front of the mirror and say he was better off not existing at all, something he read up on in *The Sorrows of Young Werther,* his favorite novel of the day . . . And so I had two men at home, my husband Francin, who was in ruins because of me, because I was beautiful and he wasn't able to come to terms with my beauty and mainly with his love for me, and my son, who suffered the very same complex . . . both those men were rather more desperate than happy when their women were by their side . . . and both of them were happiest when they were all alone with their sweethearts, when they could have them strictly to themselves, neither of them could handle someone else even looking at their women, never mind dancing with them, never mind talking to them, then it was straight to thoughts of suicide and murder, that's how jealous and egotistical both those men were . . . and in the end that first love is always a burden, always misfortune, beautiful misfortune . . .

. . . And then one day Georgine went dancing on her own, to afternoon tea in Poděbrady, and there a young man fell in love with her, a young man with a red birthmark next to one eye, and Georgine never came to our place again, and my son was heartsick, sick from not sleeping for half a year, he grew awfully thin, it was like there was a death in the family, the same sort of tragedy that befell me when that first love of mine married and on the spur of the moment I wed Francin, who loved me . . . So said Mother and I couldn't wrap my head around the fact that hidden somewhere inside the man I lived with was the young man who wrote those first verses, who was capable of such feeling, and I had to confess to Mother, that while he might have been all spit and polish back then, that's exactly why he was good for nothing, because back then he wanted too much, without ever really knowing what he wanted . . .

We were walking across the Libeň Bridge one evening and there at the Soler tram stop a woman disembarked, followed by a man, a muscleman-looking type, and right there he slapped the woman across the face. And I said to my husband, Come on, let's get going to Žertvy, never mind . . . And then a diminutive man appeared, we used to run into him on the main street, he was a plumber who went around in a pair of overalls during the day, and he had thinning hair arranged into a comb-over, pomaded and stuck to his skull, and he always wore a colorful cravat tied in a knot like some sort of painter. And come evening he enjoyed dressing up, he had an array of shirts and jackets, and always some sort of unusual shoes and brightly colored socks, and he strutted along the main street, casting about for trouble, a sort of roving avenger . . . And so there he was at the tram stop and he gave that muscleman such a shot in the face he dropped him to his knees. And although I had pleaded with my husband to get going, I couldn't tear myself away, I just didn't understand how such a diminutive person could fell that giant, who got up on one knee and wiped the blood off with the back of his hand, and when he looked at that scrawny plumber, who'd finally come across someone he could beat up, who now wagged his finger in consternation and said . . . Remember, whoever hits a woman in front of me is going down . . . well, that giant made to strike back, his face twisted in shame, that such a little man could fell him . . . but the plumber danced around and threw an uppercut to the chin and sent the muscleman right back to the pavement . . . and the plumber shouted . . . You're coming with me to the cops, they're right around the corner, you're gonna sign a statement that you hit a woman, let's go . . . And the giant got up and said . . . All right . . . and off he went, wiping the blood away . . . And that jewel of mine took it all in, he was beside himself, he'd always said hello to that plumber on the street or at Vaništa's or at The World, but had never really talked to him, until now, when he said . . . That was beautiful . . . and the plumber laughed, he resembled Polák, the footballer from Košice, he laughed and inspected the knuckles of his right hand and said . . . Mr. Hrabal, my name is Růžička . . . and then an elderly gentleman who saw the whole thing at the tram stop peeled away from the wall and as he walked past us said . . . The stuff that happens nowadays, a person should be afraid to go outside . . . And from then on, Mr. Růžička, the man who always went around Libeň in a clean shirt, in expensive, shined-up shoes, always coiffed and pomaded like he'd just come from the barber's . . . from then on Mr. Růžička and my husband struck up a great friendship . . . My husband respected this outskirts man about town, held him in high esteem, addressed him as Mr. Růžička, made him signed gifts of all his books . . . and often my husband cursed himself . . . Goddamnit, if I could only write, that would be some kind of short story, some kind of novel about Mr. Růžička . . . I often saw his wife—she was always nicely put together, always a bit rattled—shopping with her little daughter, or, as pretty women out here on the outskirts were wont to do, dolled up and strolling along the main street, stopping for coffee at Kulík's, lighting up a cigarette at the bar across the road . . . I saw when she ran into her husband, that pomaded

Libeň avenger, she always greeted him with respect, they exchanged a few words, his little daughter gave him a hug, and then Mr. Růžička continued on his way along the main street, going from job to job . . . One time the sink was clogged at Vaništa's and Mr. Růžička spread his suede apron out on a table and unwrapped his alligator wrench, his pliers, his assorted gear . . . The whole bar went quiet, and Mr. Růžička, in his spotless overalls and turtleneck, began pulling on a pair of white gloves . . . that jewel of mine called on him to say a few words . . . In my younger days locomotive engineers sported these sort of gloves . . . and at Christmas chimney sweeps wore white gloves when they brought around calendars . . . And Mr. Růžička flipped on the light switch, for a dark cloud had passed over Vaništa's courtyard, and Mr. Růžička took up those chrome tools of his, and down on his knees he loosened the screws under the sink, while Mr. Vaništa put a bucket in place, and Mr. Růžička cleaned out the drainpipe, extracted the blockage, then set to cleaning the trap . . . theatrically, so that everyone might see his work, and then he reversed the process, returned all the parts under the sink, tightened the screws . . . and he opened the faucets wide and the water gushed into the drainpipes . . . I never again laid eyes on those chrome tools of Mr. Růžička's, but whenever I ran into him on the main street with his toolkit, I could almost see those chrome tools, those implements resting there behind the leather, and I saw how it all came together to form quite the style, that outskirts style the poet Kolář so liked to go on about . . .

From the time my husband became a writer, from the time he published his third and fourth books, from then on that jewel of mine was invited to make appearances before his readers, at schools and libraries, and he always accepted the invitation in the hopes he'd get sick before the day came, or something got in the way so he wouldn't have to go. And the day came, and it couldn't be shirked, and my husband trembled with fear as he set off for his appearance, sometimes he took a train, or a bus, sometimes he even slept over, but without exception he always got the shakes and was ashen, he rambled on and said good-bye to me like he was on his way to the hospital for an operation, or to jail. I went to a number of those appearances myself, I stood off to one side and heard the fear and dread in his voice, the horror at his own storytelling, at the answers he gave . . . He never answered the question given him, maybe just briefly, but then he was off on a tangent, I felt for him, certainly as anyone who liked him must have felt for him, because my husband answered all questions, even those he should remain quiet about, those one should never discuss in public, and his voice quavered, like he was being throttled, and thus he went on, until finally catching the flow of his thoughts, and then it was like he was narrating a story, just one-on-one, and he forgot all about the audience and suddenly hit his stride, like when he wrote and things went well, everything flowing in time to his own breathing, he caught his rhythm and it took both mine and the audience's breath away, the stuff he went on about, he was even moved to tears by things he said, and right then I and everyone else in the room not only felt, but knew with certainty, that that husband of mine was number one, champion and king of the world at storytelling . . .

And only I knew that as soon as that jewel of mine gets home he'll collapse into bed and lie there in the dark staring at the ceiling, the cat dozing on his chest, my husband will lie there staring at the ceiling because he can't fall asleep, only near morning will he doze off, in a sweat over how many more people he'd promised another appearance . . . Each appearance ate up not just the one day, but the two days after, he cursed and lamented that it so rearranged the furniture in his head it took two whole days just to put it all back together. And to top it off, those two days were filled with self-recrimination, that he hadn't answered like he should have, that only now the right answer was coming to him, and I tried to comfort him, as if he'd just come from the hospital, from a battery of blood and urine tests because he was worried about his liver, and I had to reassure him it wasn't cancer, it was only cirrhosis.

My husband was skittish and fearful from all the way back in grammar school and junior high, the only reason he went into the city was for school, the rest of the time he spent at the brewery, beyond the city limits . . . he wasn't used to people, or to being inside, he was always off in a tree somewhere, or on a rooftop, always out on those endless wanderings of his, as his mother called them, racking up dozens of kilometers there beyond the brewery, alongside the river and through the meadows, as far as the Kersko forests . . . but the minute he walked into a restaurant, into a classroom, into a train car, anywhere people were pressed together, eye to eye, my husband blocked right up, just like he blocks up nowadays, when I take him to the theater, or to the movies, he always feels ashamed, like he's done something wrong, and he's as shy and bashful as a young girl, just like Mother described . . .

My husband admired people with conviction, people who could firmly differentiate between yes and no . . . my husband was incapable of saying no, he always agreed to everything, whenever anybody came over and invited him to the pub he was a pushover, even if he didn't want to go, he promised to write something with respect to their conversation, promised to make an appearance somewhere he'd rather not be, but my husband had no conviction, all he had was a feeling of guilt, and the fact he agreed to everything was his way of asking to be forgiven for even existing at all . . . I was sitting in the courtyard, my husband was off to buy some rolls, it was before noon and the sun was shining, and a young man appeared asking for my husband, I told him he'd gone to buy some rolls and the man said he'd wait, I thought he was a clerk from the insurance company on account of his suit and tie . . . Then the door slammed and my husband flew up the steps into the courtyard with his mesh bag only to stop dead in his tracks . . . he got quite the shock, and the young person standing there was delighted by the reaction . . . Are you Hrabal the writer? My husband nodded and went even redder and the young man pulled out his ID and introduced himself as a clerk from the Ministry of the Interior . . . My husband laughed and took the young man around the shoulders . . . Well, that's a relief . . . And the young man said . . . But I gave you a fright, didn't I? And perhaps for the first time in his life my husband didn't lie and said . . . And how! I thought you were here to invite me to an appearance . . . And the young man stiffened and said . . . Can we talk alone? And my husband handed me the rolls, he took one for himself and led the young man into our flat, and Ethan the cat sauntered after them. I ate my roll and through the open window heard those two quietly discussing something, Ethan the cat lounged on top of the desk, and as was his habit contributed a meow every so often as if to agree. Half an hour later those two emerged, Ethan in tow, and my husband appeared to be smiling but actually he was holding back tears. They shook hands and the young man, who wore a suit and tie and had huge, beautiful eyes like a poet, leaned over to me and said confidentially . . . No need to mention what you saw here to anyone, all right? And I stared at the courtyard tiles and didn't raise my eyes . . .

So my husband, when he was summoned to Bartolomějská Street, set off like he was going to one of those appearances of his, he left at noon and it was evening by the time he returned, and he was quite changed, even more wretched than after one of those author appearances, where he'd recently started talking about freedom, about how for him, as an author, freedom is what you make of it . . . but it was evening when he came back from Bartolomějská Street, stony-faced. And from that day forward he always had one eye over his shoulder, like a rabbi, he spoke in whispers . . . and I managed to elicit from him that the five-hour interrogation had finally ended with his having to dictate and sign a typewritten statement he'd spoken to Pavel Tigrid, that they'd been on a little outing to the country together, taken a flask along and one of the farmers out there had played them harp while they drank and discussed world politics and literature . . . And then my husband told me that starting out the conversation had been quite jovial, as he waited in the hallway in Bartolomějská Street for the elevator an officer approached and introduced himself as Captain Rarach, and said what a shame he hadn't brought along one of my husband's books to autograph, and my husband said that this place seemed quite opposite to the drunk tank, you couldn't open the doors here from the inside, whereas the drunk tank patients could leave anytime they wanted, in fact, said my husband, the doors in this hallway put even the asylum to shame . . . And Captain Rarach slammed his fist down on the table and said . . . You're not at one of your appearances or one of your pubs here! Now you're gonna make a statement about how you assisted the enemy and traitor to the republic Pavel Tigrid . . . and my husband told me what he'd dictated, and how his feeling of wrongdoing grew and grew, the old feeling of guilt at even being, combined with the additional weight of having actually spoken to a traitor of the republic . . . A stern look is what I gave that jewel of mine, who was fond of discussing truth, of saying one must always speak the truth and never fear it, no matter the cost . . . freedom is what you make of it . . .

I sat by the window on the second-floor veranda, from where I had a beautiful view of our little courtyard, where just yesterday the freshly applied plaster came crashing down off the adjacent machine shop wall, I saw our open windows and doors, saw those tendrils of grapevine cascading from overhanging wires to the tiled floor like long locks of a red-headed woman, I gazed at that little courtyard of ours, at those white doors and window frames, interrupted by great stalks of wild ivy, I heard Mrs. Beranová in the hallway below, splashing great bucketfuls of water, cursing and muttering to herself . . . And then I heard a voice, Vladimir's voice, calling to me . . . Madame, madame . . . And when I leaned over the balcony there stood Vladimir, one arm outstretched, and he really was so tall that I leaned over and was able to grasp the bouquet of tulips from him, the bouquet he'd picked in some little square in Libeň . . . I took the bouquet and Vladimir said . . . Madame, give the doctor a message that I just talked to some of the boys down at The Old Post . . . tell him the ingot mold spilled, that Mr. Fišera, who my uncle and I used to drink with at Karel's, is no more . . . in the morning, Mr. Fišera was hurrying and he tripped over a ladle and the molten steel caught up to him and almost completely burned off his legs, he died . . . he'll have a small casket! And tell the doctor what the other guy he used to work with up in Kladno told me, they brought a load of crushed cars into the scrap yard, and when they separated those flattened cars, they found a crushed human leg inside . . . Make sure to give him the message, okay? And the flowers from me are just a little token, you know what it's like, your husband's famous now, he moves in different circles, myself I'm pretty insignificant . . . And in a flash he was gone, in several strides he flew across the wet hall, I heard him strike his head on the lightbulb in the entranceway, and Mrs. Beranová give him hell for stepping on her clean floors, and on she went pouring her bucketfuls of water and splashing them over the tiles . . .

From just about the time my husband published his first book, right up to his latest, *Advertisement for a House,* his old friends claimed he had changed . . . it wasn't exactly like they were jealous, but now that he was the big writer . . . and one of those who stopped coming around was this guy who always wrote on the same subject, I forget his name now, but he always wrote short stories about those boxes on the streets that resemble caskets on biers, those boxes on the outskirts that contain tools for fixing roads and lanes, giant boxes with huge locks on them, boxes with chains wrapped around, I often noticed those boxes when the workers in the blue overalls had them open and were pulling out pickaxes and pitchforks, hoes, rakes, axes . . . This guy loved talking about those boxes and those workers, he told us that before he was a clerk he worked on cobblestone maintenance, he had his own key to one of those boxes, nothing got him going more than the contents of those boxes and the banter of the workers, when they set to with their pickaxes and hoes and pitchforks, this guy had a working-class background, he liked his beer and his rum too, but he still had better manners than my husband, he liked to sit by the window, listen in and smile, smoke his cigarette, and he always wore a necktie and when he spoke, it was inevitably of those road workers and those boxes . . . He stopped coming around to our place, I heard he died of liver disease, he wrote practically a whole book on those boxes, but the manuscript was lost and I certainly never got to see it, just like I never saw even one poem from Mr. Buřil, who hailed from somewhere in Strašnice . . . there was a rumor going around that for years he was building a huge boat in his backyard, apparently it had a stateroom and a mainmast and was so big the only way he'd ever get it out of there and afloat was to disassemble it and reassemble it again on the water.

Mr. Šmoranc stopped coming around, he was a house painter by trade and it's fair to say that next to Vladimir Boudník he was the most handsome of those poets who dropped by, women were absolutely crazy about him and I could see why, not only did Mr. Šmoranc have this curly blond hair that always looked freshly coiffed, but he knew how to put himself together, and he was always a gentleman, his model was Jacques Vaché, the surrealist writer, who lived even more surrealistically than he wrote. When Mr. Šmoranc walked into a room it was like letting the light in, his blond hair gleamed and because he worked as a painter outside on the scaffolding he was always tanned, if anybody resembled a Greek god then it was Mr. Šmoranc, who was always a bit overweight, who tried to stay in shape playing tennis, self-conscious as he was of his belly, but I knew it was unnecessary, for Mr. Šmoranc was beautiful just the way he was.

Even Standa Vávra, the printer from Horní Libeň, stopped coming around . . . Standa loved to dress well, he loved to smoke and to write poetry and short stories, he was enormously proud of his literary knowledge, he knew all the poets, from Baudelaire to Rimbaud to Breton and Éluard, and this Standa was handsome and dashing and always had a pleasant smile, and so it happened that Vladimir Boudník, during that famous phase of his, took a great shine to Standa and brought him along on those street séances of his, the ones he threw for pedestrians, for rubberneckers, for anyone interested in listening to him lecture while he copied those cracked Prague walls to his canvases and described how simple it was to turn those battered walls of Prague into a picture gallery.

Even the diminutive stagehand Paša stopped coming around, the one my husband guzzled gallons of beer with in Mr. Vaništa's taproom, they just stood there and put back ten beers, sometimes more, that diminutive Paša had a beautiful little daughter, Vendulka, he loaned her to us once when we went on vacation to the Krkonoše Mountains, she was smart and charming just like Paša the stagehand, who drank through everything he had, but he and my husband were such great friends that when they were plastered out of their minds they sat on the doorstep in front of our flat at midnight and more than once they took a nail and carved into the WC wall an oath that starting tomorrow they'd begin life anew, they'd take the cure, take their portion of Antabuse and quit those benders, because Paša was seriously starting to mess up on account of the booze . . .

My husband, from the time he became a writer, continued to celebrate those in-house weddings, but with new people . . . now it was editors and painters and sociologists coming over, but they were usually drunk by the time they arrived, having gotten plastered somewhere else, Mr. Ducháček liked to show up in the evening completely sauced, but my husband just went on making his pork roast for everyone, he made big pots of goulash and came and went with pitchers of beer, and the more everyone drank, the louder they got, they laughed and carried on, drowned each other out, even women came over, usually drunker than the men, and because there weren't enough chairs to go around, they had to lean on the wall, and some of them just went down in a heap, left a streak on the whitewash and fell dead asleep on the floor . . . Even Mr. Marysko came over, rubbing his hands together and cracking his knuckles because he still played that little cello of his at the National Theater, sometimes Mr. Ducháček even brought his pals along, and so it was that about twenty of them came over one night for an in-house wedding, my husband was all aglow, I set about getting plates for everyone, counting heads, but it was in vain because I didn't have enough anyway, and then when yet another group of young men showed up, I flushed red, took off my apron, and I got that little parasol of mine, put on those red high heels, packed my pajamas and went out into the night . . . my husband and Mr. Marysko tied on their aprons and played host to a whole building full of screaming men, the lady editors and sculptresses were coming to just as I was leaving, and my husband and Mr. Marysko handed out spoons and bread and put pots of food down on the carpet, and Ethan the tabby cat wove his way through that collection of drunks . . .

My husband went off to an appearance in Moravia, to his birthplace of Brno. The next day he returned gloomy and dejected. In the evening, when I came home from work, he sat at the table playing with a beer coaster, fingers going like crazy, he couldn't stop fiddling with that round paper coaster from The Golden Tiger. So how was it? I asked as I plunged my dirty, dusty feet into the tub. He kneeled down and lathered and washed my feet and then said quietly . . . Everything was fine, right up until I was ready to make my appearance, and standing there in the hall is this guy, pince-nez in hand, and he's with a woman, and the guy says . . . I have been entrusted . . . you are Mr. Hrabal, are you not? You are indeed! I have been entrusted by my friend, a former Austrian officer, to inform you that you are his son. And this is your sister . . . He regrets that he was unable to marry your mother back then, but he was off to the battlefield in Halič, if you please, here is a photograph showing him as an Austrian officer in uniform. By the time the war was over your mother was already married, but regardless, this is your own flesh and blood, your own father, a former Austrian officer, he's on in years now and deeply regrets what happened, but you know how it was back then, young blood for Austria . . . and if you please, here are some photographs from back then . . . And he handed me a deck of photos and I glanced at my sister, she had the same high cheekbones, the same catlike face as mine . . . Then the emcee came out of the room calling . . . We're looking for comrade Hrabal, five minutes until we start! And I stood there with my sister, I gave her a kiss, a peck like cats give each other by way of greeting . . . and my sister told me . . . Father was afraid to come himself, he didn't know if you could forgive him, would you consider coming to our place tomorrow, to say hello? And I told her I'd think about it, and then a voice came from the ballroom . . . Comrade Hrabal, if you please, we're starting . . . And there I was, in the town I was born in, at an author's appearance, just minutes after seeing my sister for the first time, and I held those worn photographs showing a man dressed in the uniform of old Austria, and as someone in the background went on about me and my work I looked at those photos, and he certainly was a handsome man, in fact remarkably so . . . but the more I looked the more convinced I was that tomorrow I would not go see my father . . . My real father, though not my biological one, was Francin, the man who raised me, the man who told me I could flunk high school every year but I'd have to get my diploma, who allowed me to go to university, and who had a terrible feeling of guilt on my mother's behalf . . . And so I didn't go, not even to see my sister . . . that father of mine in the Austrian uniform did well not to come see me, now I finally understand myself, why I always carry that feeling of guilt . . . I assumed it from my mother and Francin and without actually being guilty of anything I bore that guilt, always and endlessly fleeing before that sense of wrongdoing, which was in me even before I was born . . . and like I already told you, like Mr. Barthes says . . . Although I forge ahead, I point to this mask of mine, which I wear like an actor who has decided to play the clown, the fool . . . so said my man, kneeling before me, washing my feet, and I knew that he was my husband and I was his wife . . .

At home there in Libeň I talked to the cat more than I talked to my husband. And he learned to talk back, and to show me when he wanted me to take him in my arms. He hopped up and I took him under the shoulders, and he closed his eyes as I lifted him onto my lap. During those moments I realized what a mother's love must be like, I was overcome when Ethan nuzzled up to me, when he curled into my lap. Sometimes he dozed off, but before doing so he always gazed into my eyes for the longest time, he rested his paws on my shoulder and stared at me, sometimes he got it into his head that I needed a wash and licked my whole face clean. And now and then it was my ears that interested him, he licked them with great care while burbling sweet nothings . . . and occasionally he was already curling into my lap before he thought it over and nuzzled up to my ear and whispered something terribly beautiful. I looked forward to those moments, looked forward to coming home just as much as my husband did. Without the cat, however, the only way my husband could have lasted at home was by throwing his in-house weddings . . . Ethan tended to come home just before dawn, he always had one window open a crack, and he'd look from one bed to the other before deciding who he was going to sleep with . . . we could never tell who he'd choose. If his paws were muddy, I wiped them off with a small rag, I even wiped his belly and pretended to be cross with him, but he knew I didn't mean it, knew I was happy he'd curl up in bed with me, and so he closed his eyes sweetly and purred. And then I lay down, and Ethan the cat, when it was cold out, crawled under the covers to warm up, and then he stretched out beside me, made himself so long his hind legs reached practically to my knees. And after grooming himself he took a good long stretch and relaxed his whole body, and we fell fast asleep . . . it was always so nice, we lay there as long as we could, Ethan's little head close to mine, and occasionally we looked at each other, just to make sure the other one was still there . . . Sometimes my husband got up to have a look at us . . . Those were some of the nicest moments of our marriage, my husband standing there watching us in the breaking light of dawn, giving us a little caress . . . I saw the same gentleness in my husband's eyes that I felt for that little creature, and Ethan knew it, he was proud of the fact he had us both in the palm of his hand, he brought us happiness and fortune every day, and when one of us felt down, with great tact he was able to devote himself entirely to that person. Another charming thing about Ethan was that he ate everything we did. And if you didn't give him a morsel off your plate, then Ethan was up on a chair, front paws resting on the table, and if even that failed to get your attention, then he pawed at your elbow. Sometimes we made like Ethan the cat wasn't even there. Then he pawed at us and looked forlorn, just as he pawed at the window in the morning when it happened to be closed and he couldn't get in. And he meowed pitifully . . . and then, when we gave him a morsel of dumpling, of meat, of potato, a sampling of everything we had on the table, Ethan ate it all, because for him that food, that breakfast, lunch, and dinner was a daily test of whether or not we still cared for him. Sometimes for lunch he got his own little plate, and Ethan squatted there on a chair, front paws on the table, his little plate in front of him, and he glanced at us while he ate, and he always ate very *appetitlich* . . . I often held him up as an example to my husband, whom I bawled out for eating like a barbarian, for wolfing his food, I said just look at how beautifully Ethan comports himself, and it was like Ethan understood and he ate with such *appetitlich* style, a little cat like that pulled off everything with style. But I most enjoyed giving him his breakfast. He always got warm milk with a bread roll broken up. First he drank the milk, he stood there with his paws spread . . . and then he always stopped and turned to look at me and then at my husband, a good long look, as if to say, thank you . . . and we leaned down to pat him, and as we stood over our little cat, we looked at each other too, and couldn't help but smile, and we closed our eyes and gave each other a little head butt, just like we did with Ethan . . . And Ethan was wise to it all, we loved each other and he shared in that secret of ours, and he gave us equal time, because Ethan the cat was well aware that for us, he was the measure of all things . . .

When my husband still harbored the beautiful goal of visiting every single pub in Prague, of writing a little something about each one, he set off to Podolí, and while there he visited his sick friend, the poet Zábrana . . . but to get to the poet's room he first had to cross through a room with four old people in it, and they were so old, Zábrana told him later with a laugh, that they had about three hundred and ninety years on them combined . . . and they just sat there dressed in ceremonial black, waiting to die . . . and my husband convinced the poet that the best thing for fever and cold was to drink plenty of lukewarm beer, and so the poet, wearing only pajamas, threw on a winter coat and together they passed through that room again where those four waited to die . . . and then they stopped at Karásek's, it was still morning so my husband made sure the beer was served lukewarm, and the poet Zábrana recited beatnik poetry to my husband, he started with Ginsberg and Kerouac and on he went with the hipster angels, and they drank their lukewarm beer and chased it with shots and it was getting dark already when the poet Zábrana remembered Ferlinghetti, and so he expounded on those verses as well and they drank their lukewarm beer and downed their shots until the wee hours, when the staff began turning over chairs, and so they settled their bill and went outside, staggering under the weight of those beautiful beatnik verses—the poet Zábrana said all it took to set his head aspin was a picture of one of those beatniks—and they hailed a cab and took it to Libeň, it was after midnight already, and out there in the courtyard those shots kicked in and both of them went down in a heap, my husband called out to me, but he couldn't get up, and I was reminded of what the poet Marysko always said, my husband could get so drunk he'd fall flat on his face even if lying down . . . And so there they lay, and I was so furious I couldn't sleep, Mr. Slavíček tripped over them in his nightshirt, in vain he tried to help them up, and then he tapped on my window, but I pretended not to hear . . . But around daybreak I let them in . . . And then I was acquainted with the poet Zábrana, Mr. Honza Zábrana, whom Mr. Kolář described as a gentleman, a man who loved a bouquet of roses . . . when they'd traveled to Odessa together with Mr. Hiršal, Mr. Zábrana was the only one with the moxie to hand out bouquets of red roses to the beautiful women of Odessa, in honor of Benya Krik and the short stories of Isaac Babel. So around dawn, as light was breaking and that jewel of mine was stone cold under the table, the poet Zábrana, one leg elegantly crossed over the other, recited beatnik poetry to me, and he had beautiful eyes, and although he sat there dressed in his pajamas and winter coat, I'd never heard poetry recited so beautifully, and with such clarity, and every so often he thanked me, for here in our courtyard his fever had broken, and he had such beautiful eyes, like Charles Boyer in *Love Affair,* when he stands under the giant clock at the skyscraper waiting for his lover to appear, but she never will, because she's been struck by a car and perhaps paralyzed for life, that's how beautiful the poet Zábrana's eyes were as he recited poetry to me and my husband lay moaning under the table . . . And later that morning the poet

Zábrana kissed my hand and off he went with my husband to buy some beef and pickled herring, in order to set their stomachs right, they staggered across the courtyard, and while my husband was rather unappetizing, the poet Zábrana, on the other hand, was quite *appetitlich,* in spite of his slippers and loose-fitting striped pajamas . . . and when they got back, the poet Zábrana was fit and ready to go home, and he kissed my hand . . . while that jewel of mine lay there moaning, and despite eating some pickled herring, still felt sick . . . and presently the poet Zábrana returned with a bouquet of roses for me . . . and there in the courtyard he turned and gave me a bow . . . And my husband just lay in bed hiccupping and that afternoon we had to take a taxi to the theater because I didn't want to miss seeing *Love in the Afternoon* with Gary Cooper and Audrey Hepburn . . . For God's sake, pull yourself together, I told my husband, who staggered and hiccupped . . . the theater, near the old Hotel Kolín, past the coal yards, was so small it was like two trailers slapped together, and it was jam-packed, and barely had *Love in the Afternoon* started when my husband was overcome with hiccups . . . and the gypsies played "The Fascination" . . . and my husband got up and pushed his way down the aisle, for a moment his silhouette appeared on screen and then he ran outside, the back door opened onto a wire fence, beyond which was the coal yard, and you could hear my husband vomiting uncontrollably, just retching . . . And I, to save face, because my husband made me promise to always appropriately represent his famous name, stood up and now it was my silhouette in *Love in the Afternoon* and I turned into the bright light and told the audience . . . please excuse us, but my husband swallowed a pickled herring tail! And I sat back down, and a little while later, when the gypsies were playing "The Fascination" again on their dulcimers and violins, my husband pushed his way back up the aisle, and he squinted into the bright light and held something up in his hand and said . . . a pickled herring tail! And I yanked him down into his seat and the gypsies in the steam bath and under the showers played on with "The Fascination" . . . But when the film ended I was burning with humiliation, and the audience laughed and congratulated my husband for such a pleasant diversion during that lovely, but rather kitsch, film . . . and once again my husband showed them the pickled herring tail he'd retched up by the wire fence . . .

My husband fell so in love with the Kersko forests, he was in a constant state of rapture. And to his delight he discovered that he could throw his in-house weddings out here as well, an endless procession of weddings, whoever got married, or gave birth, or had a birthday, my husband threw a huge party with a keg of beer and bottles of booze and roast chickens and suckling pig over an open-pit fire. And within a year my husband knew every cottager and every former farmer and shopkeeper, and he even got to know the local police . . . the thing is, my husband didn't differentiate, he liked anyone who liked going to the pub, to The Hunter's Blind, to pubs in Semice and Hradištko, and as far off as Velenka, and Chrást, and Mandršejd, and everywhere he went they liked him, because my husband loved to show off, here he really was a number one and champion of the palaver, of beer drinking, and when fall and winter rolled around, my husband was invited to all the *schweinfests,* he was there first thing in the morning to watch them lead the pig from the pen, and his eyes welled up when that mallet blow or pistol shot rang out, and then he was tying on an apron and helping with the scalding of the pig, with the gutting, he loved rinsing out the intestines, and he cracked jokes and drank liquor and talked up a storm, for my husband had a bit of the farmer in him too . . . When I went for a walk through the fields with my husband he was like a king surveying his lands, he felt the maturing stalks of rye, and when the time was right he tore off a few ears and sniffed at the grain and said that in a week's time Mr. Sedláček could head out with the threshers . . . my husband knew about raising sugar beets and corn feed, and in about a year he had his own table in every one of those pubs, and he sat with the old-timers as well as the young farmers from the co-op, and he just loved talking about anything to do with work in the fields . . . And he procured a map of the area, which he marked with all the names of the local fields and meadows, and he was worked up whenever he came home with a new name . . . He was very excited with the meadow our parcel backed onto, it was ringed with pine trees and called Novák's meadow, and further along was a large field known as Loskoty and on the far side of that a stand of pine trees, and that stand was called The Brickworks . . . and the stream running through Novák's meadow continued into Olšiny, and where it emptied into the Labe was a meadow called Sezi, and my husband roamed all the way to Přerov, marking down all his favorite place names . . . the meadows by the river marshes were called Hanín, and there was a field called Jordák, and a place by the river forever known as The Giants, because of the giant oak trees that used to grow there . . . and he crossed the bridge over the river into Litole, and then walked up river until he got to a dead branch of the Labe, where the most beautiful sand was dredged for many years, and there was a public swim area too called By the Oaks, or Felinka's, my husband made me go with him once, and there in the sand was a huge oak stump, quite petrified and black and hard as rock. And same as he marked down the precise location of all his pubs in his Prague city map, so too he marked down those unique meadows, fields, and marshes in his Kersko map, not to mention the forest districts, with monikers like The Trunk, Murder, The Little Nymburk Trail, Stink Gully, Vineyard Grove, and The Pond at Deer's Ears.

When my husband was at home he sat at the table and gazed out at the alley of birch trees until the light began to wane . . . the first birch was huge, its trunk twice the size of any other, she was a beauty, with strong branches flung wide like a chain carousel, this birch, my husband said, was the same age as the others, but she was strong and brash, and therefore carved out a space for herself faster than the others, who were just as tall as her, but because they could only grow up instead of out their branches were withered and black, they put all their efforts into being slender and having more beautiful and softer bark . . . and doubtless had a windstorm come it would have toppled that giant birch tree, but a windstorm never touched this alley of birch thanks to the oak trees lining the fringes of our cottage forest tract . . . when this forest was being planted with pine trees, the rangers also planted a ring of oaks . . . Our pine forest was more than a hundred and forty years old, and when we felled one of the old trees my husband counted the rings on the trunk, and he looked at the other pines and touched their trunks and noted that some were more slender than others, that they looked to be about half as old as the thicker trees, and it was the same thing with people, he said, even when he was in grammar school, in junior high, every class had students born in the same year, some in the same month even, but some were big and some were small. And thus my husband liked explaining things to me, lecturing me, and I listened doubtfully, because the things he went on about usually seemed unbelievable, confusing, unlikely. And he liked to throw me off with those explanations, just to keep me from reacting to a particular habit of his, not that I wanted to cure him of it exactly, but I did find it weird. The thing is, he liked to go into a deep reverie, liked to daydream . . . not the sort of daydream like he was remembering a woman from his past or something, but say we were in that pine forest of ours, he'd suddenly get this dreamy look and drop into a squat and rest his chin in his hand and his elbow on his knee, and he could squat there like a Bedouin for a whole hour, eyes closed, smiling, intently focused on what he was seeing there in his mind's eye . . . And I absolutely hated this, I thought my husband was a nitwit. And out of the blue I shouted and startled him and he went pale and couldn't utter a word, as if woken from a trance . . . And I said, If you'd rather do something useful, then the doorsill needs fixing, there's a draft, and mice will get into the cottage . . . And leaning against a tree, or down in his squat position, my husband looked at me and I saw that the arrow had hit its mark, that he despised me . . . I have nowhere else left to run, he said sadly, voice breaking . . .

Come to think of it, from the time we bought the weekend cottage in Kersko and added the atelier, the attic room with the tin roof, I never once saw my husband up there writing. It was the same deal as in Libeň. When my husband wanted to write, it took him several hours to get focused, he gazed out the window, paced the courtyard, drank his coffee, smoked, didn't eat. And after a couple of hours, when he sat down to that machine of his and fed in a page, it was like he and that chair and that machine went flying through the air, above the clouds like a magic carpet ride, and he hammered at the keys, muttering to himself, and sometimes he just stared at that machine like he wanted to throw it out the window . . . And it was strange, no matter where he wrote, by the open window, or out in the yard when the weather was nice, or at the kitchen table, whoever came by and chatted him up he answered all their questions and went on writing without missing a beat, same thing when the mailman brought him some paperwork, or even a check, my husband just wrote on, nodding to himself, and people were happy to see the writer at work, except they had a hard time believing what he wrote made any sense, since he wrote so fast. They peered over his shoulder at the keys hitting the page . . . and then they nodded, satisfied, and went on their way . . . and out in the yard the kids played, a ball sailed over my husband, but nothing fazed him. Except of course if I looked over his shoulder, then he screamed as if his organ was caught in a meat grinder, as he liked to say.

And so my husband stopped writing when I was around, he was afraid of me coming home early, and here in Kersko, as soon as he saw me coming down that alley of birch trees, he froze right up and started packing away his writing paraphernalia . . . And I just waved my hand and said to him, You'll finish it off tomorrow, when I'm not here, serves you right, you shouldn't be boozing it up when I'm at work, you should be writing . . . I was quite harsh, and as a result he gave me the silent treatment and was off to wander the forest and come back tipsy, and I felt, at least for a while, that I had the upper hand. But he returned the favor by flying the coop barely fifteen minutes after I came home, into the forest he went, through the rain, to roam the meadows, the riverside, the pubs. He always returned from his forest outings—just going for a little walk, he said—late at night, when I was already in bed, and I heard him and the neighbors bellowing at each other at the crossroads, making their plans for tomorrow . . . I never locked our cottage, same as our flat in Libeň, and in summer the windows were always open and even in winter we kept them open a crack so Ethan the cat could come and go as he pleased. Here in Kersko Ethan preferred to stay home with me, curled up in my lap, he was miserable and terrified of the forest, and he only perked up once we put him in the car, and on the trip back he buried his face between his paws, if he happened to glance out at the receding countryside he was all in a sweat . . . only in Vysočany did he raise his head and put his paws on the window and look out, and as soon as we turned into Ronková Street and drove past Žertvy to Kotlaska, Ethan seemed to smile, he looked at me and nuzzled my hand, and then we arrived and opened the car door and Ethan jumped out in front of our building at number twenty-four, gave a stretch and bounded up to the courtyard, and even before we brought up our things, he was rolling around in the dust next to the hand pump . . .

I had long since mastered the tricks of the trade in that hotel grill where I worked, I made the sort of tips I never dreamed of, and even kept the purse and acted as cashier . . . I felt completely at home in that grill, having overcome my nervousness and fatigue long ago, and those patrons who visited that little grill of ours in the center of Prague knew me and called me Eliška, and those who knew me well called me Miss Pipsi . . . and we catered to all sorts, film and theater actors, directors, university students, and people walking past outside would stop and turn back when they saw those golden chickens roasting in our window . . . I was happy working here, even looked forward to it, particularly when I was entrusted with the purse, but those happy days came to an end with the arrival of a new waitress, she was full of herself and bleached her hair, she'd never done this sort of work, and the girls from the restaurant said she's the boss's girlfriend, you better watch out, but I wasn't worried, for I had worked not just in the kitchen of the Hotel Paris, but in the restaurant as well, not to mention my four years at the grill . . . but out of the blue the boss came to me and told me to hand over the purse, that tramp of his was going to look after the cash, and I was red with shame, for in our field to give up the purse meant a loss of trust. So I untied my apron and handed in my notice . . .

And so it was that a week later I landed a job as a clerk at the recycled materials plant, in the paper division, the very same shop that dispatched the truck drivers down to my husband's place of work on Spálená Street. And I, who was accustomed to the scent of meat and wine, salads and flowers, who was used to moving about the restaurant as if dancing, because I still harbored that girlhood complex of wanting to be a dancer . . . I, who was always on my feet at the grill, who stood with my right foot turned out in the first position of dance . . . practically overnight I became a clerk, with my own chair, my own desk, my own locker, my own window out to the yard, where the trucks came and went and offloaded straight to boxcars, and next to the office was a huge warehouse where ten women worked packing old paper and entire book runs . . . And I was the accountant, I logged those trucks coming in loaded with paper and books, I wrote the invoices and tallied them up in the ledger and prepared daily, weekly, and monthly reports. In a month I discovered that I had the job no one else wanted, because as those trucks and boxcars came and went with their loads for the mills, they all had to be okayed by me, everything marked down, tallied, calculated . . . a hundred and fifty invoices a day . . . and every invoice got the company stamp . . . and my signature as well . . .

And while I slipped a few rungs from my job as waitress at the Hotel Palace Grill, my husband on the other hand was flying high, he became a member of the Writers' Union and the editorial board of the Literary News, and he and Mr. Menzel wrote a screenplay for *Closely Watched Trains,* which received top prize at Mannheim, and my husband flew even higher, and Mr. Menzel received the greatest prize of all for *Closely Watched Trains,* the Oscar, and then my husband and Mr. Menzel were invited up to the castle where they received the Klement Gottwald state prize, and from then on my husband was a state prize laureate, and in fact I was a laureate too because he brought home two of those medals, and they were quite tasteful and low-key . . . And while on the one hand my husband was flying high, on the other he reached the bottom of his desk drawer, there to select something he wrote way back at the brewery in Nymburk, and assemble it into a book called *Buds,* illustrated by Vladimir Boudník, who was paid four thousand crowns for his work and promptly spent it in three days . . . And my jewel flew higher still, leveraging his appearances and newspaper and magazine articles into a book titled *Homework* . . . that's how high the state prize laureateship took him . . . nevertheless, he reached the bottom of that desk drawer of his and had nothing left, and I was curious what that laureate of mine was going to write about now . . .

. . . So in that year of '68 my husband basically stopped writing, he set out in the morning with his mesh shopping bag and went house to house, as he liked to say, to his pubs and publishers, and since I now worked as a clerk and came home in the early afternoon, I put a stop to those in-house weddings, those binges, and I was fairly fed up with those guests of ours as well, as soon as one of them caught sight of me I gave him a look that made him stammer . . . Maybe I should just run down for a pitcher of beer? And I cut him off at the knees and said there's to be no drinking here . . . Those guests even came out to Kersko, and usually my husband wasn't at home, he wandered the villages with his walking cane, and as soon as he sat down somewhere the farmers and rubes were all over him, and my husband told his stories to much laughter and everyone had a grand old time, and so my husband threw his in-house weddings in every one of those pubs, while back at our place his miserable friend sat on the bench and kept me company.

. . . But when he was named laureate, I myself threw an in-house wedding in Kersko, I rounded up all the guests and neighbors, and the booze flowed, I made hors d'oeuvres and everyone had a blast, the neighbors considered it an honor to raise a glass with such a famous person, the star of Kersko . . . and Ethan the cat lay on the bed, in a sweat, until dawn began to break and the guests made their way home, and the violin and harmonica players in the crowd lay down in the early-morning dew and played "The Fascination," à la the gypsies in *Love in the Afternoon* with Audrey Hepburn and Gary Cooper . . . and there was so much cigarette smoke in that forest cottage of ours that Ethan himself couldn't breathe, and so he ran off into the dawn . . . Before we went to bed, my husband called to Ethan for the longest time, and then he left a table under the open window for him . . . and in the breaking light of day we were awoken by a rifle shot . . . and my husband ran out, calling to our tabby, and then he searched for him the whole morning, the whole day, and we sat there after the in-house wedding bash amid the piled dirty dishes, the cigarette butts, the spilled wine . . . and there was Ethan's plate and bowl by the wall, but Ethan wasn't coming back anymore . . .

My husband sobered up and wandered those forest parcels, stopping anyone he met, and every so often he thought he saw Ethan, but it was only a rabbit, or someone else's tabby . . . all morning I just sat there, slumped in my chair, not even blinking, and when my husband came home from his searching, we looked at each other hopefully, but our little tabby was nowhere to be found. And so I just cleaned up, and then I went back to Libeň, alone, while my husband cried, he just lay there and cried, and then he went out again to wander the forests, he stayed in Kersko three more days, and on the fourth came home and I pulled back the bedcovers for him and he just lay down in bed and was sick . . . the plate and the bowl, the open window, everything stayed the same for the longest time, as if that little tabby would bound into the kitchen through the open window at any moment, I went so far as to pour milk in his bowl every day for three months after he disappeared, and every day I bought him some meat and cut it up into pieces for him, but our little cat didn't come home . . . so morning and night I took that bowl of his with the meat or milk up to the roof, where the stray cats wolfed it down, but Ethan the cat never came home, neither to Libeň, nor to Kersko. His disappearance left an awful void, it was thanks to Ethan my husband and I often held hands, or embraced, or nuzzled up cheek to cheek, for Ethan was our go-between, he connected us, brought us together at a time we thought we didn't love each other anymore, would not and could not ever love each other again . . . when Ethan paused over his bowl of milk and gave us that look, he forced my husband and me to give each other that little head butt, there on bended knee to give each other a little kiss . . .

Around that same time we went out to Moravia, to visit my husband's relatives in Ořechovičky . . . they were hosting a wedding, and every one of them had those high cheekbones, thirty people resembling one another, shot through, as my husband said proudly, with Avar and Tatar . . . introductions were essentially meaningless, because I always forgot who was who, as did my husband. And after the wedding ceremony even the priest joined in and sang along with everyone and helped himself to the food, and that clear, beautiful Moravian dialect bound everyone together . . . but I was most impressed with Aunt Hladůvka, who filled a huge laundry basket for herself with thousands of little sweet rolls from the wedding reception, but then she prepared a smaller basket of food, and I accompanied her to the cemetery, to a shining gravestone, and Auntie put a plate of sweet rolls and a plate of meat and salad down on the marble slab, and sat there for a while looking at the photograph on the headstone, a young man's photograph, and then she polished the marble slab and the headstone with great care, arranged the flowers . . . I stood there and watched Auntie sitting on the marble slab in the twilight, as if she were waiting for someone, but no one came, and her shoulders sagged, and after a while she returned the food to the basket, and shed a few tears, and then we went back to the house to rejoin the celebration . . . They told me it was her only son who lay there in the grave, six months ago he'd ridden to Brno on his motorbike to organize a volleyball tournament, and he and his bride were killed in a collision with a tram . . . And Mařa, Auntie Hladůvka, still couldn't believe it was true, that her son was dead, and every day she made lunch, took soup and a plate of food down to the cemetery, to put it on the marble slab, to sit there and wait, every day at noon without fail she brought lunch, because what if it really wasn't true, that her son was dead?

After a year passed, my husband took Ethan's food bowls from Libeň and Kersko and there in the forest beneath the pine trees lay them in a small grave, and he threw in some flowers and covered the grave over with dirt, and for a headstone my husband marked the grave with a large rock . . . Often we looked at each other, my husband and I, when we both thought of Ethan, and touched foreheads and gave each other a little kiss . . . and those moments when we kissed gradually took on a greater significance than when we first kicked off this strange marriage of ours, wherein both of us knew that although we didn't much like each other, we did somehow belong together . . . And so we returned to Kersko for the summer, unpacked our bags and our luggage and went to say hello to our birch trees and our pine trees . . . and in the afternoon I read my newspapers and magazines, now that I worked at the paper recycling plant I had my pick of any newspaper and magazine, every day and every week the trucks brought in hundreds of rejected print runs, and all of us at the plant took what we wanted . . . I sat reading those magazines with the same abandon that my husband consumed those books of his, those books he'd collected over four years at the paper salvage in Spálená Street, he read hundreds and thousands of them, but he also had a few favorites that he read over and over, and they were as worn and stained as a children's primer at the end of the school year . . . so as I sat reading a copy of *Young World* my husband walked in, absolutely thrilled, and it was obvious that he had a big surprise . . . and I looked up in anticipation . . . Ethan's back! And he gave a slight nod and took me by the hand and led me behind the cottage to the shed and he said . . .

Not quite, but he sent us kittens, three stray kittens, two of them look just like he did . . . And he brought a clean plate and poured some milk and set the plate down by the shed door and presently three little kittens came running like crazy, skidding into the plate, front paws in the milk, and they set to lapping it up . . . And when my husband went to pour them some more, all three took off like a shot back inside the shed, and when he finished topping them up back in they ran . . . to lap up the milk . . .

My husband was on a trip abroad to Germany, and Uncle Pepin waited in a casket on ice for him to return. The funeral took place the day before the first day of spring, Uncle Pepin passed away in Lysá in an old folks home, no longer aware of the world around him . . . Břeťa had long since divorced and been remarried, his new wife's name was Dáša, and she had a little girl, Danka . . . Dáša had quite the time of it with Uncle Pepin, there in the villa by the Labe he couldn't even find his way to the bathroom anymore, he woke up and didn't know where he was, he crawled around on all fours, and often barricaded himself under a chair . . . and so he lived, bedridden, in the old folks home, my husband visited him but Uncle Pepin didn't talk anymore, he just stared at the ceiling, as if beyond he could see that heaven of his . . . And so Uncle was cremated, there were two death notices, my husband had one printed up the way he wanted, there on the death notice where the verse usually goes he had them print Uncle Pepin's saying . . . *The world is so beautiful it's maddening, not that it really is, but that's the way I see it* . . . Mother wasn't too keen on that one, had a more conventional one printed, and as usual, as for a lifetime, my husband and his mother didn't see eye to eye . . . After the funeral my husband invited a whole party of guests down to Gregor's Pub, they had an outdoor garden and a bowling alley, and that bowling alley was set up with tables and chairs to handle weddings and graduations, but my husband was there to celebrate Uncle Pepin, and an hour after the funeral the mood began to lighten, people traded stories about the times they'd had with Uncle Pepin, and we drank wine and beer and ate schnitzel, and on into the night it went and that funeral feast turned into another one of those in-house weddings . . . And then my husband went on another trip abroad, and when he returned we lay Mr. Kocián to rest, he died of dementia, just gradually fell apart, and nothing could help him anymore, not even the notion that he was the illegitimate son of Count Lánský of Růže, not even his fine Schwartzenberg hunting hat and deerskin jacket . . .

. . . And before I had a chance to put away those black mourning clothes my own mother died, there in Germany my darling mother died of cancer, and when I saw her in the hospital morgue in Schwetzingen she was as diminutive in size as a little girl, my mother, who was always stubborn and tenacious, who never let anyone put one over on her, but the cancer slowly ate away at her until in the end she might have fit into a child's casket . . . And barely was I finished crying at my mother's passing when Francin's health began to wane, they operated on his prostate there in that little town where time really had stood still, as my husband liked to say, and when we arrived at the hospital they were just wheeling Francin down the hall after his operation . . . And the doctor who operated on him told us to prepare for the worst . . .

When Francin died we went to the mortuary to pay our respects, the clerk let us in, and the autopsy having been performed, Father lay there on the stone slab, he looked like a dead Roman senator, a sheet wrapped around him like a toga, and his hands were crossed over his chest and for the first time I noticed how work-worn they were, and his arms were brown, as was his face and neck, he looked like all those clerks of old Austria, white as freshly fallen snow, except for their sun brown arms and necks and faces . . . And his hands were marked with scars from those screwdrivers and wrenches of his, from a lifetime of tinkering with cars and motorcycles, and Břeťa, there with us, leaned over and kissed Father's hands . . .

Father's eulogy was delivered by the very handsome painter Hanuš Bohman, he was a friend of the family, and that painter was a revelation to me, I'd never seen a more beautiful person, never heard someone speak so eloquently . . . and then things slowly got under way at the bowling alley at Gregor's, and we ate and we drank and in the end were in good spirits, all except for Mother, who never smiled once, she just smoked and looked absolutely wretched, and that's the way she was from then on, she missed Francin terribly, only after his death did she fully realize what an incredible man he was, and how much he had loved her. From then on Mother drew into herself, she lay around the house, slept the morning through, her old cat curled up by her side, she refused everything from her new daughter-in-law, in fact started going over to the neighbor's house, the Villa Venouš, to watch TV, and she even got the idea to convert their laundry room into a little kitchen and sitting room for herself, she wanted to move out of that villa she and Francin had built together, and into a flat that at least resembled her old house in Židenice, on Balbínova Street, where she'd lived as a child and as a young girl and as a young woman, a house she had a sacramental relationship with, as did my husband. And so it happened, as per Mother's wishes, that Francin was buried, and at the head of the grave grew a large birch tree, and there we placed the urn with Uncle Pepin's ashes and lay Father in his coffin to rest.

. . . Sometimes Vladimir dropped by to Libeň, he came around more often these days, because he'd fallen in love with a young lady, her name was Věra, and decided to take her as his wife . . . And so he arranged for the wedding to take place in Krumlov on August 21, 1968, and since my husband was best man at his marriage to Tekla, Vladimir invited him to be best man yet again . . . But the night before the wedding we were awoken by the neighbors, that whole street there in Libeň was awake, as was the whole city and indeed the whole country . . . planes rumbled overhead, the Russians were landing, and then the tanks rolled in, and on my way to work I saw Russian and Polish soldiers, and there was gunfire in Prague, and a transport truck drove through Palmovka carrying a group of young men holding a blood-soaked flag . . . nevertheless my husband was set on driving to Krumlov in the morning for the wedding, but he was turned back by a row of tanks, and when he tried to drive across Štrossmayer Square, there were tanks there as well, and my husband demanded to be let through, he was on his way to a wedding, his friend was getting married, but the entire city was already at a standstill and so my husband didn't make the wedding, he picked up and went into the city center where he ran into Mr. Marysko, and they decided to attend an exhibit at Waldstein Palace, they banged on the gates and Mr. Marysko shouted . . . Open the gates! And through a chink in the gates came a voice . . . The exhibit has been postponed . . . and my husband and Mr. Marysko shouted . . . you'll pay for this, open up, it's ten o'clock, there's supposed to be an exhibit . . . !

Later that afternoon my husband parted ways with the poet Marysko, who was off to write love-struck poetry to the water lilies of the River Labe in honor of what he'd seen that day . . . and my husband, who always had to be smack-dab in the middle of everything, ended up in Wenceslas Square, where he ran into the woman who headed up the international division of Czechoslovak Writers, whose offices were now in the crosshairs of a Soviet tank parked next to Ursuline's wine bar, and that woman had in tow a wretched-looking person and when she saw my husband she brightened . . . Sweetheart, she said, I'd like to introduce Heinrich Böll to you, the famous writer, he's interested in having a look at the radio palace . . . and there was fear in her eyes, for she was a Jew who'd lived through more than her share during the war . . . and so my husband walked up Wenceslas Square, which teemed with restless groups of young people shouting Long live Dubček! and Soviet soldiers parked in *gaziks* were everywhere . . . And Heinrich Böll looked at them as at a revelation . . . *Mein lieber* Bohumil . . . just look at their hands, their faces, how muddy their boots are . . . like they just came from the front! The *gaziks* stood there and the soldiers smiled while hordes of young people waving flags streamed up and down Wenceslas Square, and from the side streets more crowds of young people flowed in and everyone shouted . . . Long live Dubček! Long live freedom . . . ! And the writer Heinrich Böll emptied packets of powdered pills into his mouth and his hands shook and he was sprinkled with white powder, and he looked, according to my husband, like a crucified farmer. And by the statue of Saint Wenceslas Heinrich Böll turned around and looked back down the square, and crowds of young people pushed and shoved their way past and Heinrich just repeated . . . Jesus Maria . . . Woe to the vanquished . . . and in sympathy my husband said in Latin . . . *Vae victis* . . . And so they pushed their way through the crowd until they made it to Stalin Avenue, where there were fewer people, but because a Soviet tank blocked the entrance to the street they had to detour through a large bullet-riddled furniture store, and my husband told me how alert Heinrich Böll suddenly became, he picked his way carefully through the shattered display case glass and broken furniture, with the deliberate steps of a soldier, he moved like a cat, his whole body tuned in . . . and in front of the radio palace there were Soviet tanks in the street, one of them with its main gun trained on the building, two others scorched and burned . . . Heinrich Böll put his hand on my husband's sleeve and said quietly . . . *Mein lieber* Bohumil . . . six years I was in the war . . . in the second wave I conquered Paris . . . and then I was on the Eastern Front . . . as a soldier I made it all the way to Crimea . . . and then back again . . . I was captured near Kolín . . . And my husband asked . . . On the Labe? *Nein* Heinrich said . . . *am Rhein* . . . I'm from *Köln am Rhein* . . . But let's keep walking . . . And Heinrich Böll set off again, and he walked with caution and stealth, like he was conquering one of those cities he and the German army had conquered during those six years . . . and so my husband and Heinrich Böll pushed their way closer to the tanks, which were surrounded by a crowd of young people who continued to chant . . . Long live Dubček . . . but the soldiers mounted on the tanks or leaning up against them were calm, indifferent, as if it was all some military training exercise, while two officers were surrounded by a group of young people who attempted to engage them in Russian . . . but the officers just responded tersely and smiled, and Heinrich Böll stood next to a burned-out tank and whispered to my husband . . . Well, if this happened with the *Heereswaffe,* there'd already be shooting and executions . . . And one of the tanks again began to burn, from the spilled diesel and gasoline . . . and the Soviet soldiers jumped up on the tank and calmly set to stamping out the flames with their jackets and blankets, and a few of them even smiled . . . and there in a pool of blood on the sidewalk lay our state flags . . . and bouquets of flowers . . . and still the officers were surrounded by a group of excited young men who went at them in Russian . . . and the officers just smiled, while the soldiers leaned against their tanks, automatic rifles in hand, or loosely slung over shoulders . . . Heinrich Böll nodded and turned around and they retreated, slowly, to the bullet-riddled store, through the shattered display case window, glass crunching underfoot . . . and Heinrich Böll said to my husband . . . Fifty years ago that dummy Hermann Hesse wrote . . . half of Europe is on the road to chaos . . . intoxicated with holy fervor she hurtles into the abyss . . . like Dmitri Karamazov . . . And my husband thrilled and said . . . Oh, little Dmitri Karamazov, that's my hero, oh, Myshkin and Stavrogin . . . And Heinrich Böll laughed and patted my husband on the arm and said . . . Myself I'm raised on, weaned on, Dostoevsky and Chekhov . . . I was eager to go off to war because I wanted to be in the mix! *Mein lieber* Bohumil, I went in as a volunteer, *als Obergefreiter der Heereswaffe* . . . and now here I stand with a feeling of guilt, feeling even worse than when I was in captivity for six months . . . now I'm sorry that back in '45 these armies didn't make it all the way to the Rhine . . . as intoxicated as Dmitri Karamazov . . .

And that August evening I stayed home, I had the stoves going even though it was warm outside, but that's when you most needed to heat our flat, on a nice summer's day . . . Vladimir's wedding in Krumlov was long since over, his now famous wedding, for there were probably tanks in the Krumlov town square as well, and Vladimir, with his self-adulation, was no doubt thrilled his wedding was tied to such an extraordinary event, and meanwhile my husband accompanied the writer Heinrich Böll through Prague . . . it was from my husband I learned that Heinrich Böll really was a major writer . . . and my husband described how they'd walked the length of Wenceslas Square, and pushed their way through Vodičkova Street, until they made it to Jáma Street, where they sat in a restaurant by candlelight and tried to drink beer, but Heinrich took only a sip—he left the glass full, my husband polished it off—because he said his liver was shot and he'd rather drink lemonade, which he used to wash down the pills from his paper packet . . . and his knees were sprinkled with white powder. And Heinrich took up the conversation, but it wasn't a conversation with me, said my husband, it was more like he was confessing to himself, accusing himself, because finally it dawned on him that the *Heereswaffe,* by losing that second war, had invited the Soviets into Prague, for a second time . . . and one day, and it won't be long, these armies will make it all the way to the Rhine . . . *Mein lieber* Bohumil, Heinrich went on quietly there in Jáma Street . . . Now I saw them, those Soviet soldiers . . . and even if all of us on the *Ostfront* had fought as valiantly as the *Löwendivision aus Pommern* . . . as the bravest Pomeranian division, *der langen Beine* . . .

then we still had to lose, because that providence to which Hitler appealed—*der böhmische Feldwebel,* as Hindenburg called Hitler either out of ridicule or because he was a fool—that providence pointed to the Soviet army as victor . . . *mein lieber* Bohumil . . . Yesterday I was a guest of Czechoslovak Writers there on the second floor . . . and today there's a gun pointed at them . . . that's history, *mein lieber* Bohumil . . . Now it's finally come to me, here in Prague . . . We started total war, and total war is what the Soviets answered with . . . *Jedem das Seine* . . . Here, now, I finally understand . . . Yesterday at Edward Goldstücker's, Pavel Kohout told me about a conversation he had with Yevtushenko, the poet . . . And how many millions of you are there? said Yevtushenko . . . and Pavel . . . fourteen million . . . and Yevtushenko . . . So there's no way you can have your own independent politics . . . Yes, *mein lieber* Bohumil, Roman law reached as far as the Roman soldier did . . . now I understand why Dostoyevsky and Tolstoy were so proud of their fathers and grandfathers for defeating Napoleon, now I understand why all Soviets, including Yevtushenko, are proud their fathers defeated Hitler . . . because, *mein lieber* Bohumil, there in Nuremburg it wasn't just government officials on trial, but even I was on trial . . . the whole country was, just like Jaspers wrote . . . *die Schuldfrage* . . . so said Heinrich Böll, bitterly, quietly, there in the Branický wine cellar on Jáma Street, and we sat in the half-light of the candles and from outside heard them chant . . . Long live Dubček . . . and suddenly the person sitting beside us rose from his table and said . . . You want a punch in the face? *Uber die Gosche!* And so we took our leave, and in the half-light of a single candle it didn't help a whit my pointing out to the man that this was Heinrich Böll . . . And we went out into the street and pushed our way against the flow of young people and waving flags, until we made it to Heinrich Böll's hotel, and there on the carpet of the Hotel Alcron we said our good-byes, and once again Heinrich Böll was solemn and downcast, he had deep circles under his eyes and looked like a crucified farmer . . . and as my husband finished telling me this I burst into tears, because I too had lived through a similar day there in Letná . . . when they'd rounded us up and beat us with pistol butts and herded us into an underground theater, where Heini and I and my parents were forced to spend a whole week . . .

Luckily I applied to the housing co-op and made my payment a long time ago, I applied right after our wedding so that one day, when the time came, we might be able to live in a high-rise and have our own WC, our own central heating, our own three rooms, small, yes, but ours nonetheless, and our own kitchen . . . but it was the bathroom I missed most, I had my very own back there in the villa with the thirteen rooms, where I'd lived with Mother and Papa and my sister Wutzi and my brothers Karli and little Heini . . . When I came home in the evening, when I unlocked my Libeň flat, I stepped into water, when I opened the door to the kitchen and the second room, water flowed down the walls, the carpet floated in water, everywhere I looked, water gushed and flowed . . . It seems that Jenda—the guy from upstairs with the beautiful bride who already ran off on him child and all because he was a drinker—was cooling down his tea in the morning and forgot to turn off the tap, and the water flowed all morning, until Jenda's father came around noon and turned it off, but we already had six hours' worth of water in our flat, in the flat my husband never wanted to leave . . . back when I showed him the application to the housing co-op he screamed like an old man . . . Never! Never! Libeň's mine! I'm staying here, I'll never leave! I opened the closets and there was water absolutely everywhere, ach, my clothes . . . ! All I had the energy for was to open up those two beautiful parasols of mine, one blue and one pink, the parasols my husband bought me when he was drunk, and I waded through the water like I used to wade through the puddles after a summer rain in Losiny, where we'd owned a villa, a summer residence, a villa long since turned into a kindergarten . . . Infuriated, I waded through freezing water that stank of lime, I threw open the windows and waded through water that reached my ankles, and after plodding around on the sodden carpets for a while I began to calm down . . . I packed my things . . . that tabby cat of ours, it was like he knew in advance about the arrival of the armies and the occupation of Prague, like he knew that his home, his bed, his window, everything he loved, would be overrun with water, that all the weddings in this house were not just postponed, but finished forever, just like those friendly armies who'd rolled in at midnight a few days ago were here forever . . . And it occurred to me that perhaps both Ethan and my papa had passed away at the right time . . . my papa, when he was dying, had this little smile on his face, like he knew he couldn't survive the arrival of those armies anyway . . .

From the moment the Russians arrived in Prague, my husband, laureate of the Klement Gottwald state prize, always expected a car to turn in off the road, to come down the lane for him, and his fear of this possibility kept him on edge . . . That's why he so enjoyed roaming the forests and villages, and sometimes he took the bus into Prague, my husband loved riding the bus, forget the car! The car was torture for him, where to park, and you couldn't have a beer, and he loathed being stuck in traffic and waiting for red lights and green lights, he fumed, and his eyesight wasn't the best anymore, he much rather rode the bus and daydreamed the trip through, he didn't like anyone talking to him on the bus, he just sat there, hands clasped, gazing out at the countryside, at that monotonous plain, and there was always something out there for him to see, something out there he agreed with, he smiled at that monotonous plain and she, as he said, smiled back. So sometimes, when the fear got a hold of him, he rode the buses, like when he heard on the radio that he and a bunch of other writers had been rounded up and thrown into a paddy wagon and taken to an undisclosed location . . . he stared down the lane leading to our gate until his eyes hurt, and when finally no one turned in from the road, when no one came for him, he took off somewhere on a bus, he didn't have to be scared of anyone on a bus, he didn't care where he was going, so long as he was on the bus going somewhere, and he read and ate his pork-fat bread, and when he reached the end of the line, he took the first bus coming back, only to ask the neighbors . . . did anyone come round asking for me? Did any car, by chance, drive up to our gate?

Those three kittens of ours—those three kittens sent to us by our dear departed Ethan—were a bit less skittish when I served them milk or meat, in fact they were even quite coquettish with me, from a distance . . . they made somersaults and curled up and smiled at me, they desperately wanted to come near, but when I reached out the fear got the better of them and they took off like a shot, and then the whole thing started up again, from a distance those little creatures gazed at me, love struck, meowed at me softly, as if to apologize, perhaps next time they would overcome their fear . . . So every day after I arrived, after my husband and I had our meal, after we had our fill of staring down the lane, I got up and went out to the shed with a clean plate, and I poured them their milk, and attracted by the sound the kittens came in and set to lapping it up with their little pink tongues, milk splashing everywhere, and I tried to fool them by pouring milk with one hand and petting with the other, but before I even got close, they shot off like fleas . . . So I gave up trying to touch those kittens, we learned to love each other from a distance, but that distance began to close after all . . . once as I sat reading I felt something touch me from behind, and by its shadow I saw it was one of the kittens, playing with the hem of my apron . . . So I started taking my reading outside and sitting on the tree stump and it took about a week before all three of those kittens were playing with my apron strings, and it was so nice to have those kittens close by, to see their innocent play, to feel them tug at my apron like a fish on a line . . . and I was sublimely happy, and my husband paused at his wood chopping to watch us, a smile on his face, for he knew that our dear departed Ethan had sent us these kittens, and that as soon as the rains came, as soon as the first snowfall, as soon as the cold settled in, these kittens would come inside of their own accord, first into the hall, and then into the kitchen . . .

Vladimir paid me a visit at the paper recycling plant, and he was triumphant, as in years past. I was amazed how that new wife had changed him, how well that second marriage seemed to suit him. But Vladimir said to me . . . Madame, did you see that gun aimed at the Czechoslovak Writers' Union? At first I thought the Russians had come just because they heard I was getting married that day and they wanted to wreck my wedding, all those tanks rolling in on account of little old me, but no sirree! They came to stop the degenerate intellectuals! How many letters I wrote them, how many petitions I sent, how many manifestos, I was the butt of their jokes at the Literary News, they refused my explosionalism, my graphics! And now they got what they had coming, now they're trapped like little mice. Thank God! And where, pray tell, is the Doctor? They say you're hiding him out there in Kersko, that he's got his own bunker, that he's scared to come out into the light, eh? I'm so glad I lived to see the day, the end of intellectual superiority! Practically like I invited them they rolled in, rolled through the Literary News like my explosions! Tell the Doctor that book of his *Buds* is being printed, but ask him what's going to happen to it once it is? Same thing that happened to *Homework,* it'll get printed, bound, but no distribution. I know it! I don't feel sorry for those thirty-five thousand copies of *Buds,* I'll even relish it when they bring them here for recycling, thirty-five thousand times seven of my illustrations, that makes two hundred and forty-five thousand of my graphic prints down the chute, isn't that beautiful? Do you know, madame, it's going to be my most glorious day, when two hundred and forty-five thousand of those little Vladimirs are loaded up here, it's going to be my greatest experience, and not because they didn't understand me, but because they pushed me away! The whole union of Czechoslovak writers, the whole league of degenerate intellectuals that printed the Literary News, four hundred thousand copies a week but never a single mention of Vladimir Boudník . . . but what's to become of the Doctor if he can't contribute that drivel of his to the Literary News, what's to become of the Doctor when they stop publishing those books of his? When the very symbol of their demise stands there on National Avenue, a tank barrel aimed squarely at that sign on the second floor . . . Czechoslovak Writer? And did you know that I'm going to have an exhibition? At the Viola! The Doctor should give it a shot and say a few words at that exhibition, he should muster the guts and come down and emcee my exhibit of graphic prints . . . so said Vladimir with a laugh, and once again he was number one and champion of the world . . .

There were all sorts of books now showing up at our paper recycling plant, leftover print runs, books cut from libraries and bookstores, books by writers who'd been written off after failing to return from abroad when our brotherly armies arrived, and books by writers who fell into that group known as writers in liquidation. My husband required a certificate from his employer, which was the Writers' Union, but since he was afraid to go down there, he sent me. I entered that very building that had the gun aimed at it for all those months . . . I came to the darkened second floor, and there in one of the rooms saw an old lady with her hair let down . . . when she noticed me she stepped into the hall and led me down to the bathroom, where she showed me a broken chain on the toilet and was disappointed to learn I wasn't from the plumbing outfit, that I was here to get a certificate from my husband's employer, and she told me that she used to live here, and now that the writers were moved out, she had her old room back again. And I looked into another room, a young woman sat there, and when I told her what I wanted she called through an open door . . . Can we issue a certificate of employment for Bohumil Hrabal? And a man's voice came from the other room . . . Never. Bohumil Hrabal belongs to writers in liquidation. But I wasn't about to let it go . . . So give me a certificate he's in liquidation! And the young woman stopped smoking for a moment and called out again . . . Can we issue the laureate a certificate he's in liquidation? And an older man in a checkered Esterházy suit appeared in the doorway and told me to go to the liquidation fund, there on the top floor of Práce Publishing on Wenceslas Square, that's where I should make my inquiry, the clerk there fixes watches in his spare time and otherwise issues certificates for writers in liquidation . . . and the man in the Esterházy suit added . . . you see, now it's our turn to drive around in Saabs . . . and I just said . . . good-bye now, have yourselves a nice day . . . And I went outside and crossed the street to Ursuline's, the tank was long gone, but as far as my husband and I were concerned it was there still . . . And then I found the address on Wenceslas Square and the elevator took me up to the very top floor, which seemed empty, but then I found an attic room, and true enough, it gave me quite the start, a man sat there behind a desk, a watchmaker's loupe in one eye, and I told him why I had come and who had sent me, and the man went on tightening the tiny screws of a pocket watch with a tiny screwdriver and then he said . . . Not a chance, to obtain his new ID, Bohumil must have a certificate of employment . . . but these days that sort of certificate is not issued to a writer in liquidation . . . writer in liquidation doesn't qualify as employment . . .

I had one of the electricians at the paper plant fix my old vacuum cleaner, and my husband stopped by in the little station wagon to pick it up . . . The same day I just happened to issue an invoice for practically a whole boxcar full of Škvorecký's *Lion Cub,* it was on its way to the paper mill in Štětí, and around the time my husband stopped by for the vacuum cleaner, a hundred copies of a book called *Happiness,* written by a man named Stránský, were dropped off . . . And I said, who's this Stránský? And what's his *Happiness* all about? And my husband perked up . . . My god, that's heaven sent, I just saw him yesterday, he runs a gas station in Karlín, what an unbelievable coincidence! I said to him, listen, loan me a copy of *Happiness,* I want to compare it to Mr. Pecka's books, he was in the lockup too . . . And Stránský's pumping gas into my car and says . . . The thing is, my friend, I've only got one copy of *Happiness* . . . and that's on loan to a friend in Slovakia, and it's practically falling apart . . . And so there at the paper plant we took the old vacuum cleaner out of its case and filled the case with all one hundred copies of *Happiness* . . . and we set off for Karlín . . . and my husband brightened . . . Look, this Stránský is nobility, his family had a château! If he was just a touch more handsome he'd look like me! And *Happiness* . . . that's about his time in a prison labor camp . . . and he's a number one and a champion because he doesn't cry about it, he faces it square on, just like Mucha in *Cold Sun* . . . that's about a labor camp too . . . but look out! He's a man about town! And then I saw Stránský there at the gas station, and once again I regretted that my husband didn't know how to dress, Stránský stood there pumping gas, and he had a thick black beard and an air of nobility as he pulled out the cash purse, and I said to myself, I'm never getting gas anywhere else . . . And those two writers in liquidation were already waving at each other . . . and then my husband was beside him, and the contrast was awful, that jewel of mine, ever since we lived in Kersko, really did look like a hick . . . and now Stránský came around to the window and I offered him my hand, that jewel of mine always grabbed a woman's hand first, but Mr. Stránský, thanks to his proper upbringing, knew he must wait until I offered him my hand . . . and his lips grazed the top of my hand and he bowed . . . precisely the way the officers kissed my hand when they used to come around to our villa . . . and my husband opened the trunk and removed the heavy case . . . and he hauled it over behind the pump, someone else took over pumping gas for a while, and there behind the pump all I saw was a green trunk lid come up . . . And then it started! Mr. Stránský ran out from his Saab, yelling and waving his arms, circling the pump, and everyone watching thought he'd lost his mind . . . and then he ran back and disappeared under the trunk lid again . . . and back he came, this time yelling something at me, I guess he wanted to thank me . . . he kissed my hand and slobbered all over it . . . and then he ran into the office, yelling all the way, and collapsed on the couch . . . And that jewel of mine threw the empty case on the backseat and climbed into the car and his eyes were closed as he squealed with laughter . . . If only you'd seen it! When I dumped those hundred copies of *Happiness* into the trunk . . . Something awful!

Vladimir stopped by to visit me at work, he wanted to show off the new outfit his mother bought him, he turned circles in the office like a model, he pulled up his pants leg to show me his new socks, and he had a new sweater, and he even wanted to undo his fly and drop his pants to show me his new undershorts. But all of that was just a pretext, before he could calm down, catch his breath, and tell me the real reason he had come . . . Madame, I'm going to have an exhibition . . . And where is your exhibition going to take place, Vladimir darling? At the Viola. A whole series of graphic prints, the last set of monotypes . . . Madame, as you make your bed, so you must lie in it . . . that husband of yours, the Doctor, he could emcee my exhibition, but the Doctor now belongs—where? To writers in liquidation. And why? Because the armies came in to stop the degenerate intellectuals, to stop them not just from publishing the likes of the Literary News, but all those books imbued with—what? The same degenerate attitude . . . tell your husband, the Doctor, if he likes he can stop by on Tuesday to see my exhibition . . . so said Vladimir, turning circles again like a model . . . And people will see things that'll make their eyes roll back in their heads, my explosionalism is sweeping the world, they know about it everywhere, at an exhibit in Miami they said I'm ahead of the Americans by two years, further along than Pollock was . . . they know what's what, and in France an article came out about me, it's just here they know nothing about me, and that's because who held the reins? The degenerate Literary News . . . But now all the writers in liquidation are crawled under a rock and I have free rein, now no one's looking over my shoulder, no one can stop me from showcasing my explosions, my vibrations, from showcasing the stuff that's thousands of years old yet newborn at the same time, I've merged Altamira with socialist explosions, I'm going to put on an exhibit in the very shadow of the Soviet tank barrel, the one that had Czechoslovak Writer in its crosshairs . . . And after Vladimir left, the women in the office couldn't get back to work for at least an hour, just a few taps at the typewriter here and there, they were thunderstruck by Vladimir, he really was a drop-dead handsome man, with his curly hair perfectly coiffed into a chestnut wave . . .

But Vladimir wanted to be an even bigger champion of the world, even more famous . . . neither that tank aimed at the Czechoslovak Writers' building nor that wedding of his was enough . . . and perhaps the reason those secretaries of ours were driven to such distraction is because they felt he was capable of anything, even murder had I shown a trace of doubt for that exhibition of his at the Viola . . . and maybe they felt he even wanted me to doubt him, because then he could drive a knife into me oh so easily, slit my throat, choke the life out of me with a silk rope, and it would be effortless, for such was his anger and suppressed rage . . . And one morning I told everyone at work what my husband had told me, that on the day of his exhibition at the Viola, Vladimir placed an ad in *Evening Prague* announcing my husband as emcee . . . but he didn't give my husband any such message, he only asked timidly if my husband planned to come see the exhibit . . . And meanwhile his wife had a get-together down at The Patron with some former classmates . . . And at the exhibition Vladimir gave away those graphic prints of his, but nobody wanted them, they weren't interested . . . and then some intellectual asked Vladimir if he was familiar with Vitězslav Nezval's decals? And did the name Mathieu ring any bells? Because if so, then Vladimir was the epigone . . . And so Vladimir showed up drunk to The Patron, where his wife's former high school classmates were whooping it up, a bunch of twenty-somethings . . . And one of the guys asked Vladimir's wife . . . Is this your father? Tell him to pull up a chair . . . And through the laughter Vera introduced Vladimir as her husband . . . but her classmates went on pretending he was her father, they made fun of him, and Vladimir tried to shout them all down, he stood there singing his own praises—he and his explosionalism were number one, he was a world-class fellow—but his wife's classmates were simply in hysterics, and Vladimir, pale and ashen, was cut to the quick . . . And so there he stood at The Patron, alone against a drunken class of aging high school grads and his own wife, who took Vladimir's most deeply held beliefs for a joke . . . And Vladimir went home and tied a noose around the door handle, he assumed somebody would come, but no one did and Vladimir hanged himself, he killed himself, assuming that someone would come and untie him, as they had countless times before . . .

. . . My husband delivered the eulogy standing over Vladimir's casket at the crematorium, he shouted like he was at the bottom of a well and clutched at the paper from which he read his short speech . . . my husband shouted like he was lost in a forest . . . Vladimir! You clicked at the pale horse and now here it is! And that's how Vladimir left this world, my husband's great friend, and the two of them loved each other so much it's a wonder they never killed each other . . .

. . . My husband said after the funeral . . . And the only real champion of the world was Vladimir, now I see it, now when he's saddled up that pale horse I finally understand what it means to be a number one . . . only Vladimir! Now, when he's gone, I finally understand that everything he worked on, those graphics of his, and everything he wrote, those manifestos and manuscripts, that was all Vladimir through and through . . . and that's the way it should be, nothing was above his explosionalism, no philosophy, no psychiatry, no literature, not even any politics, nothing was stronger than that which he considered his absolute, his heaven . . . And that's the way it should be, even though Vladimir knew of Joyce and Becket and Eliot, of Salvador Dali and Picasso . . . that was all beneath him, had to be beneath him, because he had the inner strength to become a number one, to elevate that rather plain field of graphics . . . that's why he looked down on me, why he despised the literary types and all the literary papers, because he was his own god, while all those literary types, to whom he wrote so many letters, so many manifestos, all those editors, to whom he sent dozens of his graphic prints in order to prove his worth, not one of them had the decency to reply . . . and that's why he was spiteful, he knew the tank barrel pointed at the Writers' Union was his revenge, that gun was like his own finger, pointed at his enemies, because Vladimir wanted to live life even larger, wanted to soar even higher . . .

The rains came to Kersko and brought along some happiness. Not only did those soaking little kittens allow us to pet them when they were at their milk, they even let us pick them up. So I diligently wiped down one little kitten after the next, they always kept me company, and I was most happy when all three of them were in my lap, purring, giving me those little head-butts, and my husband stood there watching and smiling, those kittens made him forget his fear for a while, it was such a holy picture, a holy family . . . when the cold weather arrived it forced those kittens, one by one, to come into the kitchen, and once they were there warming themselves by the stove, once I brought their bowls into the kitchen from the shed, those kittens were ours. The first one inside was the tabby cat, we named him Ethan, then came Cassius, black all over, and then there was little Mánička, the most skittish of the three. Everything those kittens did was determined by Ethan, the other two always waited to see what he would do first. And so when we turned off the lights and outside the rain poured down, Ethan was always first on the bed to settle next to my husband, followed by Cassius and then Mánička, who liked to sleep down by our feet . . . like the Moravian poet we were friends with who loved telling us he was from a large family of blacksmiths, and that as the youngest and smallest of six siblings all sharing the same bed he slept down by their feet, just like our little Mánička. That lead tabby cat had eyes just like our dear departed Ethan, and he too was in the habit of staring into our eyes so intensely he'd force us to look away. So when we returned from Prague, when the kittens had all but given up on ever seeing us again, when we drove into that lane of ours, Ethan was the first to come greet us, the first into the kitchen, and the first with the courage to jump into our laps and give us that little head butt, and only then did the others follow. And Ethan was first to lap his milk and first to eat, and he'd pause in the middle of eating, turn around and look at us, as if he wanted not just to thank us, but to take our measure . . . Each kitten had its own place, Ethan sat next to my husband, Mánička next to me, and Cassius had his chair by the stove . . . And come evening, when my husband was off to the pub—he had to go to the pub every night and come home when I was already in bed—I read my magazines and washed the dishes and tidied up, and no matter what I was doing those kittens kept me company . . . Those kittens didn't know how to play, they seemed not to have the time for it, only when I made them a paper pigeon on a string did they play for a while, but it was more like they were trying to make me happy . . . the thing is, those kittens had a melancholy nature, a constant fear we would leave them here, all alone . . .

. . . My husband took some planks and a few bricks and built a sort of roost behind the stove, next to the warm wall, and each kitten had its own plank, they never fought over anything, Ethan had the top, Cassius the middle, and the bottom went to Mánička, who had this sort of Chaplin-esque personality, always cheering up her brothers and me and even herself, she was so charming and diminutive, like Chaplin in those films of his. And the cats had this beautiful cleaning ritual, first they cleaned themselves and then took turns cleaning each other so thoroughly with their little tongues, I could just watch them at it forever . . . When my husband came back from the pub, he almost always came back with Mr. Franc, they were out there hollering at each other on their bicycles, you could hear them from way off, didn't matter if they were coming from The Hunter's Blind or from Hradištko or Semice, and they lingered in front of the gates bellowing about the rain and the humidity, they argued about whose address was whose, like a couple of drunks . . . and then my husband came in, and he stood there swaying and said . . . Darling, are you asleep? Mr. Franc says hello, and the barkeep says hello, and Franta Vorel says hello, and even Mr. Hamáček says hello . . . and when he lay down, Ethan was first to hop onto the bed, and then came the other two kittens, and after midnight my husband got up to let whichever one of those kittens wanted outside, he staggered around and let those kittens in and out, never uttered a word of complaint, never swore, because he said those kittens were like our children, and children when they're little are sacred . . . even if they are good for nothing, said my husband the state prize laureate.

. . . And again my husband was summoned down to the local committee in Libeň, summoned by the same rude young man who got such a kick out of asking him what should he list as employment on his new ID? And my husband wanted to go back to baling old paper, because a writer in liquidation doesn't qualify as employment, at least not according to the young man at the local committee. And that evening we had a visitor, and when my husband saw the *gazik* pull up outside, the army vehicle with the tarp on back, he rushed to grab a pair of underwear, and then another, but I yelled at him . . . Yeah, that's right, you moron, you laureate, as soon as they catch you they're gonna strip you down and make you change into their outfit! And then he made to escape through the window, but the *gazik* was already parked at the gate, so my husband bailed out through the attic, down the stairs, into the forest, through the fence and to the pond, where he hid among the thick branches of a weeping willow . . . and then I ran down to the pond and called out to that laureate of mine that it was just his friend from Ostrava, the one who edited the *Red Blossom* . . . He was on his way to Prague, where he landed a job as a crane operator, and he just stopped by to let my husband know he was alive . . . yes, it was true he'd been hogtied and thrown into a sack and driven who knows where, but after three days they let him go again, and the worst of it was when the crew of the *gazik* stopped at a pub, five hours they were in there drinking while he, Kubíček, lay trussed up in the dark, but at least he was alive, he said with a laugh . . . meanwhile my husband looked outside at the *gazik* and grew paler and paler, but Kubíček laughed and said . . . That isn't the *gazik* they carted me off in, that one's mine, I've had it five years already, it's a rust bucket, only does fifty K, but the family and I use it on weekends . . . well, I guess I'll be going, I just stopped by to let you know I'm still alive and kicking, Bohumil, though that sack was pretty uncomfortable . . . I'm glad I could stop by here to tell you about it . . . but keep on writing, you know how it is, I'm not as tough as you are, but what can I do? I can't change the way I am . . . And he stuck out a huge hand and he was a formidable man and he had a honey-colored beard and a big honey-colored smile, and you could see that smile as he moved off, he was a country fellow with a rickety sort of walk, and then he started up the *gazik* and turned into the road, and my husband was on tenterhooks if anyone saw that *gazik* parked at our place . . . he said . . . he could've parked a bit further down the lane, so as not to be seen from the road, you never know, the cops are always coming through here . . . and I said to that laureate of mine . . . Just be careful you don't shit your pants, sweetheart . . .

. . . I phoned the local committee in Libeň to learn that the young clerk who was giving my husband such grief was on vacation, so I thanked them and sent my husband down the next day, and I told him to bring along a couple of his books because there was a woman there . . . And so in the afternoon that jewel of mine showed up at my work, waving his new ID around and he was happy and full of laughter, and as always when he was happy he had a runny nose, and he wiped the snot off on his sleeve in front of all the secretaries and exclaimed . . . Man, have we got handkerchiefs! And I flushed and apologized on behalf of my husband, it was the country living that had ruined him . . . but Boženka, with whom I had a running argument about the arrival of those brotherly armies—she screamed it was good, I screamed it wasn't, she screamed I should go to Germany and take the doctor with me—this same Boženka now said . . . No big deal, I know the Doctor, when he worked here he never had a handkerchief, always wiped the snot off on his sleeve! And my husband said . . . This is true . . . and he gave everyone a Russian-style bow from the waist . . . And suddenly he wasn't a writer in liquidation anymore, suddenly, for at least a moment, he was once again number one and champion of the world . . . And he said . . . So I walk in and the clerk asks what can she help me with, and I tell her I'm here to pick up my new ID, and that my name is Bohumil Hrabal . . . What, she can't believe her eyes, Hrabal, I'm so glad to meet you . . . And she turns around and finds my file and pulls out my ID and says . . . anything missing? And I say . . . just a little thing, the employment . . . And that clerk sits down and begins to write and says . . . For God's sake, every decent person knows that . . . Writer! And what a writer, I've read every single one of your books, but my favorite is . . . *Private Storm* . . . And she hands me my ID . . .

The first one who didn't come home was Ethan, the one who so resembled our famous Libeň tabby . . . Cassius and Mánička went into the night, calling out in their special code, listening, they searched for Ethan in the shed and in the forest, but their leader never came home again, and those little cats were heartbroken. And then Cassius didn't come home, it was three days before my husband found him in the neighbor's woodshed, strangled, he was used to jumping up on the woodpile there through a slatted fence, only he hadn't noticed the extra slat nailed on by the neighbor, and so he hung there by his little throat until he died. My husband dug Cassius's grave at the base of a pine tree, threw in a primrose blossom, and then covered the grave over and marked it with a log.

In spring the police in their fatigues swept through the Kersko forest parcels, trying people's doors and windows, as they did every year to make sure there were no break-ins or squatters . . . My husband sat at home, looking out at the lane through the branches, when suddenly three men in fatigues appeared. And before they got to the door my husband almost kicked the bucket, for he thought the police were coming for him, just as they had come for Kubíček, the editor of the *Red Blossom,* he thought they were going to truss him up in a sack like a piglet and drive around for a couple of days before letting him go . . . But they simply came to ask if we had all our stuff and if anyone had tried to break in. And my husband was so overjoyed they hadn't come for him that he rolled out the red carpet, offered them vodka, wine, put on coffee . . . and the cops asked him what he was working on and my husband lectured them on how it was most important for a writer to write nonsense, without nonsense he'd have neither this cottage with the atelier, nor a car, and he went out of his way to accommodate those young people in their spattered fatigues and he made them some more coffee and poured them a few more shots until, startled, the cops noticed the time, and they asked again if everything was in order at the neighbors' cottages, and my husband assured them he'd been living here with his wife the whole time, that nothing had happened all winter, because all the cottages were connected by a path, everyone had a gate to it, and my husband regularly wandered those six forest parcels along the path, and weekend and holiday cottagers used the path to visit with neighbors, they didn't have to walk the road, where there were too many cars . . . And he probably should have kept this to himself, because the lead cop pulled out a map and said he had to mark it down, the path was unreported, it might be used by saboteurs hiding out, he had to go check the path for himself, he was going to mark it down in his map of the Kersko region, because if something happened, like convicts on the run, or soldiers going AWOL, then at least the cops would be familiar with those escape routes that might make the monitoring, chasing, and capturing of criminals more difficult . . . They took their leave and went off to inspect that path connecting the forest properties, and then a shot rang out at the far end of the path, and when they came back the lead cop stopped at the gate and said . . . Everything checks out, just managed to shoot a stray cat is all . . . And he pulled a revolver from his pocket and my husband said that must have been a hell of a shot, to hit a cat with a revolver on the first go, just goes to show the lead cop was a champion and a number one at shooting . . . And when they left, when those three men in the mottled fatigues faded back into the forest, my husband found Mánička there on the forest path and in the afternoon he buried her . . .

. . . And, as promised, my husband took me to the Hamáčeks', where we always went for *schweinfest* . . . We rode over on our bicycles and this time the occasion was smoked meat . . . And the hoopla, the shouted greetings, and it was Saturday and Mr. Hamáček and my laureate kept scurrying off to see if the smoked meat was ready yet . . . And we chatted away and every time Věra, Mr. Hamáček's daughter, passed through the living room to the kitchen she grabbed a schnitzel from the bowl atop the sideboard and ate it with such relish that we too had to dip into the bowl every time we went to check on our husbands . . . and at last Mr. Hamáček and my husband came in and that jewel of mine was grease-stained and cheeks glistening and Mr. Hamáček dumped the first huge bowl of steaming smoked meat onto the cutting board . . . and as master of ceremonies, Mr. Hamáček invited us to dig in . . . Mrs. Hamáčková, however, with her bad gall-bladder, couldn't even look at smoked meat, she held a dishtowel up to her face and turned away and went on sipping her tea and nib-bling her biscuits . . . and next to the cutting board was a plate of grated horseradish and apple and jars of cream mustard . . . and Mr. Hamáček's grandsons dropped by and his brother-in-law too and all of them ate quite *appetitlich,* small portions with bread on the side, and then there was my laureate, who just had to be champion . . . he laughed and wolfed down chunks of smoked meat, nothing on the side, and he threw back his head and cried with delight . . . In all my life I've never seen anything more beautiful . . . Oh this pork butt trimmed with fat . . . And this little offering, smoked pork belly . . . And Mr. Hamáček gestured and said . . . And how about a riblet . . . or a little tenderloin . . . ?

. . . Before morning my husband started making trips to the bathroom, and that's where I found him, on the floor, in the fetal position, clutching his side and moaning, and blaming it all on race, just like Mr. Marysko . . . What's the matter? I shouted. And he lay there twisted, folded up like a jackknife, and wheezed . . . We horrible Slavs suffer from gluttony . . . I'm such a fool, such an idiot, such a dope . . . And he tried to throw up, he tried to sit on the bowl, but he just collapsed and screamed in pain, around 4 A.M. he staggered off to bed and just lay there, cursing himself, and even cursing Mr. Hamáček for giving him too much smoked meat . . . And I yelled at my husband that he was the swine, he shouldn't have stuffed his face like that . . . And before noon that champion of mine lay there still, pleading for the good lord to take him away, and I laughed and swore at him, told him it was his punishment for being such a glutton . . . And around noon he started turning yellow . . . Doctor Štork had a cottage here in Kersko, and I rode over on my bicycle, and when Doctor Štork arrived he pulled back my husband's eyelids and pronounced . . . Jaundice, tomorrow you come to the clinic, but now it's Sunday, and there's nothing more to be done . . .

At the general hospital by Charles Square the doctors were in a bit of a quandary. All morning they couldn't decide whether my husband suffered from a ruptured gallbladder or viral hepatitis. And so my husband sat here, still wearing the same clothes, tongue-tied, thunderstruck, surprised and caught off guard. And he had a little smile on his face, but it was a resigned smile, for it dawned on him that sitting here at the clinic was a balancing of the sheets for all those *schweinfests* and smoked pork hocks, for all those drinking binges, why from the time he was a kid he drank everything he came across, if there was a party he poured the dregs together and before his mother could return from seeing her guests off that little sonny of hers even poured himself a cup from the bottle, and then drank it in secret, and liked it . . . During the five hours he sat here, he replayed all those in-house weddings of his, tallied up those Olympic-size swimming pools full of beer, that freight train of pork meat, those cisterns of hard liquor, and in the end he wasn't even surprised to be here at the hospital, because his balance sheet was now in the red, because by rights he should have kicked the bucket a long time ago, should have died of cirrhosis or stomach ulcers or a heart attack . . . And when the nurse made her rounds with lunch for the patients my husband got a plate of mashed potatoes, and he sat in the hallway like a tramp, like a wayfarer of old, and tucked into his mashed potatoes . . . and he raised those eyes at me, I knew that look, those kind, guilty eyes, like when he felt ill in the morning, when he went to throw up, when he couldn't, as he said, expel that pickled herring . . . I stood over him and just couldn't help laughing, the laughter of a wife whose predictions had finally come true, how many times since we were together had I begged him, screamed at him, quit drinking, you'll see, it'll make you sick! Don't drink so much, control yourself! Go take the cure at Skála, I don't want to be a widow, but if I have to, then shuffle off while I can still remarry, die of the drink while there's still time . . . I could fill miles of cassette tape with all the talking I'd done, almost every day I yelled at my husband till I was blue in the face, but it was like talking to a brick wall . . . But for all the yelling I did at my husband for his drinking and his in-house weddings, I saved the worst of it for myself, I kept rehashing everything, an interior monologue, as my laureate called it, that went on for hours . . . how many times had I told myself I was going to leave that drunkard, but then I always remembered his mother, and what she had suffered through with him . . . anytime there was vomit anywhere in Zálabí, or yelling late at night, the neighbors were over like a shot the next morning to complain to Mother about her sonny, indeed for years after he left that little town they still complained, that little town, as he liked to say, where time stood still . . . only to find himself in Libeň, on the brink of eternity . . . And now here he sat, all yellow and mortally afraid of having to go to the hepatitis ward, where he'd be cut off from the world for six weeks, cut off from any visitors . . . But then a young doctor came in and ordered my husband, for about the tenth time, to lie on his back, and with both hands the doctor probed all around my husband's stomach, and then he plunged his fingers down as if into bread dough . . . and announced . . . A stone the size of a ripe walnut! And he called for Doctor Štork and the attending physician to come have a look . . . and Doctor Štork said . . . Bravo, a gallstone, well done! As big as a ring of keys . . . And the young doctor was off again and Doctor Štork said to me . . . You might as well go home, he's going to be here for three weeks, we'll see what happens when his color begins to improve . . . Nurse! Issue a hospital gown, and room number 204 should have a free bed, we had a patient die there yesterday . . . complications of the liver.

. . . And then I left, I didn't know what to do, I cried not for that laureate of mine, but for myself, for the prospect of being alone, I guess at the end of the day having a drunkard husband beats being alone, like having a problem child beats having no children at all . . . I was feeling quite sorry for myself as I walked through the clinic courtyard. And I entered the corridor, and there beneath the big clock sat a gurney with a sheet stretched over what looked to be a body, and there was no one around, and I don't know what got into me but I touched the sheet where the head was, the cold human head, and it made me remember something Mr. Marysko told us, how, without even knowing why, he'd tapped on his father's head as he lay in the coffin, and I don't know why either but now I tapped on the head under the sheet, and the clock above the gurney said four thirty and a neon light shone overhead . . . and suddenly I knew that lying there was the person who had died in the very bed my husband would soon occupy . . .

I went to the hospital every day and always wore my nicest outfit, just the way my husband liked, those red high heels and those parasols, one day red, one day blue, and I bought myself another parasol, a green one, and off I went to see that laureate of mine in the hospital like I was going on a date. And my husband lay there on his back, arms splayed, tubes stuck in his veins, he was getting the intravenous drip all day, like it was Rainbow Bleach, designed to bleach the yellow out of him and return him to some normal skin color. And beyond the window the old trees reached right up to the third floor, and in the branches nested turtledoves, and my husband lay on his back, the medicine dripping into him like some sort of distillate, like cognac . . . and my husband smiled, he seemed almost happy here in this room . . . and the first thing I saw when I walked in was a tall man who reminded me of Gary Cooper . . . he was dying of liver cancer . . . And sitting on the bed by the window was a man sniffing suspiciously at a slice of black forest ham, like he wanted to throw it away . . . but in the end he ate it, with disgust. And across from him was an enormously obese man, his liver was on the fritz too, and he kept going on about the same thing, how as soon as he gets better he's taking everyone down to the Smíchov brewery, where he's assistant brewmaster, and he and his friends are going to drink a whole keg of beer . . . And there was a man who'd suffered a heart attack while gardening, he lay there in bed, condition unchanged, lay there and it was several days since he'd used the bedpan, because he was embarrassed . . . And instead of being down in the dumps, my husband adapted right away, because everyone around him was worse off than he . . .

. . . So he lay here for three weeks and I visited him every single day, and I always wore those same red high heels, and I sat by my husband's bed and gave him his digestive biscuits, which he washed down with lukewarm tea, and the intravenous droplets kept coming, like it was diluted alcohol dripping into his veins . . . and how many times did I hear from one of the patients, when they followed me into the hallway, that they rued the day my husband had to leave, because then who would tell them stories late into the night? And I assured them it wouldn't be too soon, since my husband had a gallstone the size of a ring of keys . . . And so every day several IV bottles drained into my husband, he poured hectoliters worth of lukewarm tea into himself, ate bushels of digestive biscuits, but that jaundice refused to back off, showed no sign of giving an inch . . . Once when I stopped by, the Gary Cooper fellow had visitors, two sons and a daughter, beautiful young people glowing with health . . . they came to see their father and bring him some goodies from the *schweinfest* . . . there was blood pudding and white sausage laid out on the bed, and a thermos full of barley soup on the table . . . and the kids stood at the head of the bed, talking quietly to their emaciated father, they offered him blood pudding and white sausage but he turned his head away . . . and his kids smiled kindly, they were artists of the flying trapeze, as their dying father had been once upon a time . . .

And my husband was falling apart because he was in the hospital for three weeks and because he'd probably need that gallbladder operation to remove the stone as big as a walnut . . . Meanwhile, I accepted an invitation to accompany two friends of mine, Lothar and Pavel, to Hrabyně in their Mercedes . . . they were wheelchair bound and needed me to help with the wheelchairs in and out of the car, and just generally over the weekend. For those two friends of mine, simply getting into the car required Herculean effort. First Lothar rolled up to the Mercedes and opened the door, then he grabbed the roof with one strong arm, wheelchair tight up to the car, and then he mustered all his strength and swung his body in, and he was all in a sweat, but he smiled and with relish lit up a cigarette from his stash in the car . . . And I folded up his wheelchair, I did everything according to Lothar's instructions, removed the nickel-plated footrests and pulled up on the handles attached to the leather seat and the wheelchair folded right up . . . Pavel and his mother loaded up the trunk with bags and suitcases, and a box of presents, and Pavel double-checked to be sure they had all their tools and a spare canister of gasoline . . . And then he opened the door on his side and rolled up tight to the car, and he too gripped the roof of the Mercedes with one hand and the headrest with the other as he swung himself into the front seat . . . and I folded up his wheelchair as well and attempted to stow both chairs in back, but it wasn't as easy as I thought, the boys had to coach me at it, and Lothar turned around in his seat to give me a hand, and then he warmed up the stereo cassette and James Last played "The Chorus of the Hebrew Slaves" from the opera *Nabucco,* and Pavel said good-bye to his mother and the Mercedes started quietly away, and it was amazing because all the foot controls, gas, brake, and clutch, were adapted to function as hand controls, and Pavel drove and positively glowed with pleasure, while Lothar puffed on his cigarette, and both men smiled, both men wore colorful T-shirts covered in Honda and Suzuki logos, and Pavel wore a baseball cap, like Formula One racers and pit crews wear, with a Norton logo on the brim, and now James Last played "Liebestraum," and Pavel clowned around as he drove, out of the blue he stuck a finger in Lothar's cheek and twisted, and Lothar jerked his head away, in fits of laughter, and scolded . . . Leave me alone!

And Lothar swapped tapes and the melancholy piano of Jiři Malásek began to play, fingers lightly tripping over the keyboard . . . "Harlequin's Millions" . . . and I thought about what my husband told me last week at the clinic, with respect to the brewmaster, the one who planned to invite everyone to the Smíchov brewery once he got better . . . just before midnight the door to room 204 opened . . . and the brewmaster leaped out of bed, wide-eyed . . . and as he stood staring into the open doorway he shouted . . . So you've come for me! And he took two glass urinals and smashed them together, and wielding the shards he shuffled slowly toward the door, arms outstretched, and cried . . . So come and get me, I'm not going to make it easy . . . and my husband and the other men in the ward raised themselves up in bed and stared at the brewmaster and at the doorway and my husband saw Death standing there . . . but the brewmaster didn't let up . . . So come and get me, take your best shot, come on! You're scared, aren't you . . . ? and then the brewmaster turned around in the open doorway and said to those terrified patients . . . And he's gone . . . and he threw those glass shards away . . . and gave a victorious smile . . . and then he collapsed . . . and when the doctor came in he found the brewmaster dead . . . He was a helluva guy . . . my husband said . . . And the melancholy strains of Jiři Malásek's "Harlequin's Millions" played on . . .

And so we drove through Hradec, and then through the mountains, and down the other side, and James Last kept us company, and the two friends clowned around and laughed and talked about where they should take their holiday next year . . . And I couldn't help thinking about my husband, lying there in a building by Charles Square listening to his liver . . . And out of nowhere Pavel says with a laugh . . . When I used to race I was good, and a nice guy to boot, but as soon as they pinned the number on me, no more mister nice guy . . . on the track, all my friends were my mortal enemies, and it was the same for them, we yelled at each other, told each other to go to hell, and the minute someone passed me he was my archenemy, because as soon as my number was pinned on, I was champion of the world . . . One time when we were racing for the Marketa Prize, my friend passed me, and I caught up to him and we were running side by side, neither one of us wanted to give an inch, foot peg to foot peg, on top of each other for a whole lap . . . and then bang! My friend shot off, somersaulted away in a puff of smoke . . . and I do another lap, and he's lying there on his back, his bike off in the bushes somewhere, and I'm saying to myself the next time I come around he'll be back up on his bike, but I make the next lap and he's still lying there, and the lap after that . . . and the flag waves the end of the race and I come in second, and I should be happy with second place, but all I see is that friend of mine lying there, how I kicked at him and he lost control, because he was kicking at me, to make me lose control . . . And so I ride over there and put my own bike into a skid and it's on my butt I slide to a stop next to my friend, and I'm shaking him, yelling into his ears, just desperate, and then my friend opens one eye and I say . . . You bastard, you're not dead? And he sits up and I say . . . You're not busted up? You SOB, all those laps you had me worried you were lying here unconscious . . . And he laughs and says . . . You know how it is, the bike's kaput, and for every minute I'm unconscious—I get a hundred crowns! So said Pavel with delight as he piloted the Mercedes, and the Mercedes obeyed his every command . . . Pavel hardly ever touched the brakes, he surveyed the road ahead as far as the eye could see, and then he drove like he was playing the violin.

Pavel glowed with luck driving along in the Mercedes, the Mercedes that gave him a chance to forget he'd been trussed up for the past eighteen years, as he described himself . . . Meanwhile, back at the hospital by Charles Square, that jewel of mine was frozen in fear at the prospect of having an operation and simply going home . . . where everything would return to normal . . . but no doubt, as I knew him, he was preparing his last will, and changing it daily, aghast at the thought, what would the world do without him?

Pavel said with a laugh . . . And we were on the way to celebrate my win, and there in Slapy I took a corner at a hundred and thirty, I knew immediately I'd pushed it too far, and the machine went down, and I knew I had to kick it away, that's the main thing, my friend, because when you wipe out it's you and the machine flying along together, but she got ahead of me and then waited for me and slammed into my back . . . and then the hospital, and the doctor, and my father leaning over me . . . You're going to walk, you're going to walk . . . but I just lay there, and my friends came and went with flowers . . . Within a year you'll be walking . . . the doctor told me, trying to cheer me up, but first I had to go to Kladruby . . .

That jewel of mine often said to me, during his pub days . . . Ach, those blues of mine, those little hurts, that wish to slip into the void . . . trivial, when I think of Pavel and Lothar . . . those boys all trussed up, and I never saw them anything but happy . . . not that they are, but the kind of stuff that eats away at me, they got over a long time ago . . . they focus on the pleasures of life . . . on wanting to live . . . And me, ach, what a coward I am . . .

Pavel overtook a transport truck, and when the road ahead was clear again, he twisted a finger into Lothar's cheek, who was changing cassette tapes . . . For God's sake, Lothar shouted, quit it, you know I'm ticklish . . . And Pavel laughed and went on . . . And in Kladruby, all it took was one look around the room to realize how bad off I was, in every bed a cripple like me . . . The nurse instructed me to take her around the neck when she leaned over . . . And then she carried me to a wheelchair and said she's going to teach me how to use it . . . And back then I said . . . And when are you going to teach me to walk? And she lowered her eyes and said . . . First we'll teach you how to use a wheelchair . . . And I said . . . But the doctor told me you were going to teach me to walk here! And the nurse said . . . Your abdominal muscles are much weaker now . . . you'll see, tomorrow we'll teach you how to swim, swimming makes patients feel much better . . . So I went about learning how to use the wheelchair, and the nurse strapped me to the backrest to keep me from falling out, and she told me to grab hold of the wheels and try to roll forward on my own . . . Don't be nervous, Lothar . . . And I got the hang of it, I learned to back up and even pop a wheelie, I liked being mobile, beating at the tires, spokes drumming across my fingers, and one time I almost took out the very nurse who taught me how to use the wheelchair, she was standing by the front doors, and I came flying in and just short of her hit the brakes and the momentum threw me forward and I headed face-first for the pavement, but the nurse caught me and we went down together . . . But Miss Eliška, the most amazing thing is, in my dreams I'm never paralyzed, even after eighteen years in a wheelchair it's like that, in my dreams I always see myself walking, never once in a wheelchair . . . but before the full import of this thing hit me they took me swimming . . . the nurse carried me there and lowered me into the pool and it was beautiful, I always loved to swim, you know, I grew up near water . . . I loved to swim, still do, but back then, when the nurse lowered me into the water, that's the first time I felt it was probably all over for me, I dragged those legs of mine behind me, and it was only in the water I really felt what a wreck I was from the chest down, and as I swam I looked up at the ceiling, at the droplets of condensed water raining down, and I cried as I dragged my wasted body behind me . . .

Meanwhile that jewel of mine strolls the hallways of the hospital by Charles Square, preparing for his operation, and he wanders around, not in any pain, he can even watch television if he likes, but that laureate of mine is terrified, frozen in fear . . . surely he's forgotten that when he's at his lowest all he has to do is remember Lothar and Pavel, who never whine and complain, though they've been wheelchair bound for all these years . . . but I guess over there by Charles Square my husband plain forgot all about them . . .

. . . But Pavel, Lothar said . . . we first met in Kladruby, I was there with a shattered spine, and Bibi was there too, it was a car accident that brought him in . . . And we rode around in our wheelchairs, and went swimming, and even rode down to the pub, all the time waiting for some miracle cure, because no one had given it to us straight yet, we still had hope . . . And this woman would come from Prague, she was some sort of artist, and there in studio she taught a whole legion of cripples lace-making and crochet . . . So I learned to lace-make and crochet . . . And one day Pavel here is supposed to learn to use this wired knitting frame, it's like a little harp that lies across your knees and comes with all sorts of colored thread, and in walks the chief physician and asks how the new work is coming along, how do we like it? And Pavel says . . . But when are we going to walk? And the doctor says there's news from America and Russia that they've learned how to reconnect severed nerves . . . And Pavel threw the knitting frame to the floor and shouted . . . Do something for me! You expect me to spend the rest of my life embroidering rugs? Shortly thereafter we were invited to the chief physician's office, all of us excited, talking over each other, figuring he was going to tell us when they were going to start reconnecting our nerves, and the boys were praising Pavel, for now they'd give it to us straight . . . And then the door opened and the doctor walked in looking like he'd been out on the town all night, and he looked at the floor and said quietly . . . My friends, I've only got one thing to say to you . . . All of you are healthy! Except that you're never going to walk again . . .

. . . We drove through Opava, and soon the Mercedes turned onto a secondary road and then we stopped in the main square of the modern little town of Hrabyně . . . And as I had folded up the wheelchairs earlier, I put them back together again, and suddenly Pavel and Lothar were surrounded by dozens of wheelchairs, all their friends had come out to welcome them, obviously everyone was waiting for Pavel and Lothar to arrive.

And everywhere I looked in this little town people in wheelchairs were coming and going. At the gym I saw a man, a former body builder, according to Pavel, who'd been paralyzed in a car accident on his way to pick up a trophy for best body . . . but here he was, almost as if nothing happened, working out with weights, he lay on his back as more disks were added to the barbell, he could bench press a hundred and fifty kilos and was training for the championship, there's nothing he wants more than to win, said Pavel, and every morning he was out rolling through the countryside in his wheelchair, and he watched what he ate and drank in order to be at his best . . . There was also a basketball court at the gym, and the young men whirled around on their wheelchairs like acrobats, they stopped on a dime and popped wheelies and threw baskets, and sometimes they crashed and toppled out of their wheelchairs, still throwing baskets as they went down, and the nurses helped them back into their wheelchairs and the game went on as before . . .

Pavel entered the sixty-meter wheelchair race, as soon as his number was pinned on he got this fierce look in his eye, and when the starter pistol went off he dug in with all his might, his wheelchair practically shot across the starting line, and then the racers pounded away at the tires and drove their wheelchairs toward the finish, and a young man passed Pavel and Pavel's face twisted in anger, he crossed the line in second, while behind him two wheelchairs got so tangled up a wheel flew off and the riders went down in a heap . . .

Lothar, surrounded by friends, headed straight to the pub . . . I wanted to give him a hand, but Lothar made it from wheelchair to barstool just fine, and he drank his beer, and his friends listened to him with interest, because he was from West Germany, where he'd lived for ten years now . . . Lothar's wife left him because he was a paraplegic, and after she'd gone he decided to take advantage of the fact he was German born and move to Bavaria, to the town of Marktheidenfeld, and it was a good thing, too, because now he drove a Mercedes and always brought back a little something for his friends in Hrabyně, not to mention that every year he donated a brand new wheelchair . . . I never met more courageous men than these two friends, who'd asked me along because my husband couldn't make it . . . no doubt had my husband gone, he would have spent the whole trip talking about his horrible bad luck, about that looming gallbladder operation . . .

. . . And then came the main event, the sixty-meter race, and the competitors flew across the finish line, and again Pavel took second . . . and then the nurses handed out laurel wreaths and the winner got a big bottle of Alpa aftershave . . . I saw Pavel congratulate the winner, but he had the look of a mean horse . . . And competition continued in discus and shot put, another race wound its way over the institute trails and through the little town, it was a hard-fought contest with everyone involved, except of course for Lothar, who sat in the pub with friends, and the conversation was pretty much one-sided now, a Lothar monologue, where he went on about anything and everything—supermarkets, his little house, his stay at the clinic in Murnau where he went every six months for a checkup . . .

. . . And on went the monologue, and then Lothar handed out these stylish new calendars to everyone, myself included, and Lothar told me I didn't have to stick around anymore, because he was with his friends, and he didn't really feel like dinner, because when there's drink to be had, you don't even need to eat much . . . And I flipped through the calendar, there was a different painting for every month of the year, created by artists who were wheelchair bound, and some of them were not only paralyzed, but missing limbs as well, as I saw from the accompanying photographs, and those paintings showed the beautiful countryside, pastoral scenes without a trace of melancholy, only joyfulness at the landscape and the flowers and the fruit trees and the ocean and the little hillside towns, and the shepherd with his sheep, and the fisherman returning with his catch . . .

And I looked around that small pub at Lothar's friends as they listened to him, and they had these fixed smiles . . . while back on Charles Square my husband wandered the hallways, and come evening chatted with people about his writing, and for those worse off than he, my husband was champion of the world . . . but the only reason that jewel of mine told his stories late into the night was to keep his mind off the possibility of dying during that operation, or of suffering after, like his grandpa and Uncle Bob, both of whom had passed away from cancer . . .

Pavel invited me to come visit a friend of his . . . so we parked in the basement garage and took the elevator up to the seventh floor, and when I helped Pavel out of the elevator I said . . . Mr. Hiršal told me that the first time he brought his mother from her village of Chomutice to Prague, after they rode the elevator up to his flat on the top floor, she said . . . Pepíček, why'd we have to go in a little closet before coming into your flat? Good one, said Pavel, and we rolled down the hall and all the doors to all the rooms were open . . . and all the beds were made, everything neat and tidy, apparently everyone was off watching the races or shopping or down at the community center . . . Through an open door I saw a young man sitting in an armchair, beside him was his wheelchair, and he had tired, feverish eyes . . . Hi, Pavel said . . . and the young man whispered something I couldn't make out . . . And Pavel rolled on down the hallway, and someone came out of their room in a wheelchair, sunlight glinting off the nickel plate and spinning spokes . . . And Pavel said quietly . . .

The first year is the worst, before a person calms down a bit and comes to realize what's happened is his fate . . . with me it took about two years to sink in, and like most I thought I might be better off just putting an end to it . . . it occurs to me my friend's probably down at the pub, he loves his beer, when he puts back his six beers he forgets everything else, he's king of the world, and, as your husband likes to say, number one and champion of the covered courts . . . You've seen yourself what we have to go through, the whole routine, just to use the bathroom . . . But look here, don't worry about it . . . the thing is, we've got a little device, we pee in a tube and it goes into a bag attached to the leg, and it's got a little tap on it and it's good for about six hours . . . but that's nothing . . . like I already said, it's those first two years, when you're learning to use the chair . . . before you get the hang of it, ach, the beating you take . . . you're rolling along and it's like you're running from yourself, but inevitably that chair catches up to you to remind you . . . And down at the pub, if you don't look too hard, it almost seems like you're in a regular town . . . but soon as someone in a wheelchair has to go use the bathroom, then you notice not just the chair but the condition of the person in it . . . ranges from those who have a spinal injury, to those who in addition are missing a leg and might have a claw instead of a hand, and then there's those missing both legs and both hands, and then of course even those who have the vertebrae in their neck broken, and must wear a brace, of the sort worn by Erich von Stroheim in *Grand Illusion* . . . And Pavel stopped at the elevator and I leaned over his shoulder and pushed the button and on the way down he laughed and said . . . Last year when we were at Lothar's place we took the Benz to Wertheim to visit a friend of ours who's also in a wheelchair . . . he got his motorcycle caught under an American tank, and it wasn't just his spine destroyed but all his nerves as well, and so all he had left was his wife, who wouldn't desert him, and the use of his chin . . . he had an electric wheelchair that he controlled with his chin, steered left, right, and so forth. And on the way back home in the Benz Lothar and I shouted . . . We're kings . . . kings!

And there in the hospital by Charles Square, whenever he felt like it my husband could go out to the hall and have a smoke just like everyone else, and whenever he felt like it he could run down to the little convenience store where the psych ward used to be . . . and if he wanted he could watch TV, or wander out to the courtyard, to the little wall that backed onto the monastery garden and the magnificent baroque church . . . and across the street soared the spires of Emauzy . . . but alas there on Charles Square my husband was paralyzed with fear that he might have cancer, the same sort his grandpa and uncle died of, and he was so despondent they had to send a psychologist to comfort him and buck up his courage, my husband, of all people, who so liked to dish out free advice to anyone worse off than himself . . .

And perhaps because Pavel knew my husband felt down, knew he was seeing a psychologist there in the hospital, he took me along to see the workshops at the rehabilitation center, just to give me a little perspective to take back . . . Out front we ran into that bodybuilder, the one paralyzed in a car accident on the way to pick up his trophy for best body, he came barreling down the hillside path at full speed, mud flying off the tires, and he stopped so fast the wheelchair lifted off the ground, and he popped a wheelie, and the sweat dripped off him, and he was a good-looking man . . . And I said to him . . . How are you? And he said . . . Pretty good, madame . . . And he popped another wheelie and spun in place like an acrobat and said . . . This wheelchair here has nothing to do with me anymore . . . the future's mine! I'm cross training now . . . going to smash the world weightlifting record! And he reached out his hand to Pavel, more like high-fived him . . . and he spun around and with a surge of strength spurred that wheelchair back up the hillside, where the setting sun glowed behind the trees, and he pummeled those tires, arms flying like he was swimming the butterfly . . .

And we went inside the workshop, to the office, and Pavel introduced me to the director, who was also in a wheelchair, and when he reached out to shake my hand, he had to use his left hand to support his right . . . And then we rode down a long hallway, there were several plastic-covered couches along the walls, and at the end of the hallway was a glass partition, behind which a number of young women sat in their wheelchairs, and the setting sun threw their silhouettes against the wall opposite, and the women smoked voraciously and the smoke swirled behind the glass and rose into the leaves of a large overhanging ficus . . . and the doors to the workshops were open and I pushed Pavel's wheelchair along and behind us the director said quietly . . . Here we give it two hundred percent . . . And inside a large workshop young women in wheelchairs worked diligently at the machines, they wore white caps over their hair, and when they saw us looking in, they paused for a moment to give us a nod . . . and the scene repeated itself in each workshop, women in white caps bent over their workbenches, tools in hand, assembling what looked to be radio components . . . and the director said to me quietly . . . the caps are made of organdy, for not a single hair must get into the diodes . . . And down at the end of the hall the sun had set and the shadows grew longer, and we turned around and went back, and harsh fluorescent light spilled from the workshops into the hall, and that light made the shadows even deeper, and now a worker in an organdy cap rode over to one of the couches in the hall and spun her wheelchair around in such a way that she just slid onto the couch and lay there on her back, arms splayed, taking a break . . . And the director showed us to another workshop, where an engine purred softly . . . two young people worked here, but they weren't in wheelchairs like the others . . . they lay on their backs on a four-wheel stretcher, and that stretcher was parked under an overhanging panel of sorts, like when you slide under a car to work on the chassis . . . And these two young people lay on the stretcher, focused, working away with their screwdrivers on the panel overhead . . . They give it three hundred percent . . . the director said quietly . . . this work is a lifesaver for them . . . And we made our way outside and said our good-byes, and again the director had to support his right hand with his left when he reached out to shake my hand . . . And then I pushed Pavel along in the wheelchair, and the lights of the market and the restaurant and the cafeteria and the pub shone below, and the billboards and apartment buildings were aglow with light, and there was the fluorescent glow of the workshops we'd come from, and lamp lights dotted the sandy trails, and for a moment it appeared this town was just like any other . . . Pavel turned around and said softly . . . The director has MS . . . one arm he can't use anymore, and he's in constant fear of losing the other . . . And I so wanted my husband to see what I had seen, my husband there on Charles Square, paralyzed in fear by a plain old gallstone . . .

I was to stay overnight with a married couple, they lived in an apartment building and were confined to wheelchairs as well . . . I arrived late, their child was already in bed, and the scent of anise filled the apartment . . . the young couple was getting ready for a trip tomorrow, they said I should excuse them while they got ready, and the young woman sipped Prostějov rye and offered me a glass as well . . . When I went to wash my hands I noticed how everything was within arm's reach, there was a child's tub hanging from the ceiling on a nylon rope and pulley, and the rope was secured with a cable clip, sort of like a lift line in a theater . . . And I took my time, washed my face and hands . . . The young woman appeared in the doorway, trailing the scent of anise, and said . . . Would you care for coffee or tea?

And I thought of my husband, of his predilection for blabbering on to people who were at death's door about life's final moments . . . and that first week in the hospital he practically fell apart, they had to send around a psychologist to sit next to the bed and drone . . . Imagine what it'll be like when you can leave the hospital after the operation, when you can get up in the morning and have yourself a little shave, and a little chat with your wife before she's off to work . . . you'll get your breakfast ready, tea with a little lemon, a buttered roll . . . and you like to read, so when it's nice out you'll open a window, and maybe stroll down to get the paper, nothing finer than having a leisurely read of the paper . . . and the prospect of this scenario horrified my husband all the more . . .

I walked into the kitchen and the young woman was using a hand grabber to take a sugar bowl from the cupboard to the table, and then she rolled her wheelchair over to the kitchen counter, where she prepared tea into a Meissen cup and saucer . . . And she lit up a cigarette and smiled while I sipped my tea and she asked me what was playing at the Prague theaters and what books were being published . . . and I had to tell her I didn't know . . . and then the young woman told me that she was an athlete, that she'd attended the Paralympics in Heidelberg and come in second . . . and she gestured to her second-place certificate on the wall . . . and she told me she worked as a secretary for a magazine that represented disabled people from all over the world, and that she was training to compete in javelin at the next Paralympic games . . . and her husband packed their suitcase and checked their sleeping bags and smiled as he wheeled through the kitchen and living room into the hallway, past their sleeping child . . . and I looked through the open door to the bathroom, to where the plastic child's tub hung from the ceiling on a nylon line . . . and beside the toilet, two nickel-plated handles were bolted to the wall, and I couldn't imagine what this couple had to go through before doing something as simple as sitting on the bowl . . .

Again I was reminded of my husband, coming apart at the seams there by Charles Square, to the degree some young psychologist was sent around to whisper in his ear . . . And when you're recovering, you'll go down on your own to the cafeteria for lunch, and you'll pick something from the menu that's good for the gallbladder . . . and then you'll have yourself a nice meal, eat nice and slow . . . and then you'll stroll back home . . . and there's parks with benches all over Prague, and you'll have a seat and watch the world go by . . . and then slowly on home to bed, because lying on your back is good for a recovering gallbladder . . . and then! You've got a radio, so you can listen to concerts . . . and the news . . . and then you'll wait for your wife to come home and tell you all about her day, everything she chatted about with her coworkers . . . and then you'll prepare a nice dietary dinner together . . . and then it's back to bed and you can watch TV . . . but look out! No blood and guts . . . A recovering gallbladder hates gunfire . . . crime shows have the same effect as pork hock . . . so a series of beautiful days lie ahead, when you're home after your gallbladder operation . . . And later on, when my husband told me what the psychologist had said, I saw how convinced he was that it was all over . . .

As we were getting ready for bed, we heard loud voices and music out in the corridor . . . and then a knock on the door and the young woman went to open up and it was Lothar and Pavel . . . come to say good night . . . and when the door closed behind them we heard a crash in the corridor . . . and the young woman went back to take a look and said . . . No big deal, Lothar dropped his radio . . . And then all was quiet in the apartment, I lay in bed staring at the ceiling, muted music and song and excited voices drifted in now and then, and I just couldn't get to sleep, my mind buzzing with everything I'd seen that day . . . until finally, exhausted, I managed to drift off . . .

And early next morning I helped the young couple load everything into their car, even the crib with child, and a couple of javelins . . . and as with Lothar and Pavel, it took almost half an hour to help get my friends settled, to get everything, including the wheelchairs, stowed away in the trunk . . . and we said our good-byes . . . And then I knocked on Pavel and Lothar's door . . . they were up already, James Last playing on the radio, Lothar splashing on some cologne, and both my friends were well rested and full of laughter as they sipped their tea . . . And back and forth to the elevator we went and I carried the bags and suitcases, and when we finally had everything packed, my friends swung themselves into the Mercedes and I folded up the wheelchairs and stowed them in back, and Pavel was behind the wheel again and when we drove by the community center everyone waved and Pavel honked and Lothar was moved that his friends were waiting for him, that they came out to say good-bye, that even though he lived way off in Germany now they still considered him a friend, he was, after all, born here, schooled here, married here, even disabled here, divorced here, before finally ending up in the paralysis ward here . . . And once we hit the state road Lothar cried . . . Floor it, Pavel! So we can make it home early . . . and he went on about his life, how he was in the army in Prague and served as a castle guard, how he was a hell of a bodybuilder, and how he made money on the side bouncing drunks at Fleck's Pub . . . and look here, he said, who do I owe for this Mercedes? Zdeněk, husband of a schoolmate of mine . . . he saw me there in the paralysis ward and said there's no way we can leave him here, especially after his wife ran off on him, we're going to take him home with us, he'll die here otherwise . . . and Zdeněk was a party chairman . . . and so he saved me and I put myself back together at his place . . . and in about half a year I moved to Marktheidenfeld to be with my mom and sister . . . and today I've got this here Benz . . . but you know, we didn't have it easy . . . Pavel, tell us one of those funny stories about your old man, I love hearing them . . . you know, it ended badly for my own dad, he spent two years in one of Hitler's concentration camps because he was a social democrat, and at war's end he came home absolutely wretched, on the very day our cows were taken from us . . . and the day after it was more of the same, they came and took our kitchen and our shoes, all they left us with was a teacup . . . and they relocated Dad and then he died there in Germany . . . a real comedy, eh? Hey, Pavel, tell us about the time your old man and his friend were at the butcher's *schweinfest* in the gymnasium in Žižkov, how they hung from the rings at midnight, flew over the buffet tables . . . Pavel, tell us how they hung from the rings by their feet while playing their trumpets . . . "Sixth of July on the Strahov Ramparts" . . . and people dancing on the gym floor watched them glide back and forth, don't you remember? Well, there you go, I certainly remember the story, and that second trumpeter was named Špírek . . . I remember, because when I was in the army I used to visit the Špíreks' . . . and that must have been beautiful, flying around up there playing trumpet, I can see it now . . . and do you know what beat all, Pavel? You really don't remember? It was when they played . . . "And My Baby Gave Me a Rose" . . . and then crashed into each other midair, trumpets and all . . . and Špírek knocked out two of your old man's teeth and your old man knocked out one of his . . . That must have been beautiful, Pavel, too bad I wasn't there to see it . . . And Pavel twisted his finger into Lothar's cheek again . . . and Lothar laughed and cried . . . Pavel, leave me alone, man, you know how ticklish I am . . . And I smiled and dozed off in the backseat . . .

Monday afternoon, as I was preparing to go see my husband, the phone rang and there he was, telling me in a broken voice that the operation was over, that he'd gone downstairs on his own power to call me and tell me the operation was a success. But that wasn't entirely accurate. Yes they'd removed his gallbladder, but when I got to the hospital I saw he had a catheter and plastic bag attached . . . and every day over a liter of fluid drained into that bag. And he lay there, still hooked up to the IV, and he shared a room with six other patients, some of whom were post-op as well, but while they got to eat mashed potato and compote after forty-eight hours, my husband was still on biscuits and tea after three days. That plastic bag was a humiliation for him, an awful burden, like he was anchored to his liver, and there he lay, while his roommate, Engineer Hrdina, also post-op for gallstones, was well enough to sit by the window. This engineer gave my husband grief. The first time my husband saw himself in the mirror after the operation he was startled by that yellow face of his, and he glanced around the room to see if anyone had caught his reaction . . . And sure enough, Hrdina had and said . . . Awful, isn't it! And when my husband held his glass urinal up to the light, in hopes of seeing some improvement in the color of his urine, which was still as dark as black beer, Engineer Hrdina exclaimed . . . A catastrophe! And when the nurses brought around lunch, and then dinner, and everyone but my husband got mashed potatoes, Engineer Hrdina said . . . That doesn't help raise the spirits, does it!

. . . But it was Doctor Štork who delivered the greatest blow to my husband . . . the third day after the operation he came to my husband's room, and he was quite excited and said in a cheerful voice he'd attended the operation personally, that Professor Baláž himself had performed the operation and it was unanimous, such a beautiful red liver as my husband's they hadn't seen in a long time. Except of course he didn't know my husband, who thought this was a ruse designed to mask the real truth, because why else wouldn't they give him any food. And so my husband got up and wandered the hallways and dragged that plastic bag around, he sat there in the hallway with his face in his hands, thinking the worst of thoughts. Professor Baláž himself came around, that most handsome man who resembled Harold Lloyd, and he took off his spectacles and leaned over my husband and looked him in the eye and said . . . Whatever it is you think you have, you don't, understand what I'm saying?

When I arrived on the fourth day, my husband lay there in a fever, not even hearing me anymore, for he'd lived through an awful afternoon . . . A group of student nurses was making the rounds, they were about to graduate and had their uniforms and their white caps and were in line to receive their Red Cross badges, but they still had a final series of exams to perform in the ward where my husband lay, they were to go from bed to bed to demonstrate on actual patients what they had learned . . . After which the head nurse tested them in theory as well, behind a hospital screen brought in to provide privacy for the head nurse and student nurse being tested . . . And so it happened that after the head nurse finished testing all her students, and giving them their grades, the screen was simply left by my husband's bed . . . and when my husband opened his eyes he saw that screen beside him, the sort of screen placed around a dying patient's bed, the sort of screen Mrštík's novel began with . . . *Bring in the Screen* . . . And my husband spent an hour behind that screen, and even after the nurses removed it, there was no convincing him it wasn't the sort of screen put by a patient's bed when he's dying . . .

And Sunday came around and Mr. Hendrych stopped by to visit my husband, and he could hardly contain his delight at seeing my husband laid up as he was, with his catheter and plastic bag . . . Mr. Hendrych was jealous of my husband, convinced he was the better writer of the two, whenever he dropped by Libeň they engaged in endless conversation about art and literature, and they must have logged hundreds of kilometers together through Čimický Park and Ďáblice Gorge, and as usual this Mr. Hendrych talked of nothing but himself, he refused to even acknowledge any other writer, he was incredibly impressed with himself, and before anyone else could chime in on the subject he claimed that he was now the champion of Czech prose, the king of central Europe and rightful heir to take the scepter from my husband, who'd been written off . . . So said Mr. Hendrych with a laugh and he sat there, one leg thrown casually over the other, and as he laughed and delighted at his future it was all too much for my husband, who fell into a fever after Mr. Hendrych left, and in the evening they had to give him oxygen because his temperature shot up to thirty-nine degrees, and every single doctor on duty stopped by, because that fever was nothing to be taken lightly.

And that same evening the professor came by to announce that my husband must have an X-ray, and then we'd see . . . And my husband went for an X-ray of his liver and just stared at the ceiling, the ceiling peeling plaster like puff pastry, that's all he did these days was stare at the ceiling, perhaps so he wouldn't have to see anything else, and his friends stopped by on their Saturday visits and chatted and brought along fruit and bottles of beer, but here in post-op my husband ate only what the doctors gave him, baby biscuits washed down with tea, and all he was interested in was what Engineer Hrdina had to say from his bed by the window . . . and his urine was still dark and the visage in the mirror still awful, and when he tried to shave, the razor fell from his fingers he was so weak, which prompted Mr. Hrdina to say . . . The weakness of a scattered soul!

And Saturday night, when my husband had all but given up the professor was coming by, there he was. He walked into the room, X-ray slide in hand, and he took off his glasses and said to my husband . . . You plan on wearing that bag forever? and he laughed. And my husband said . . . No, no, not really . . . And the professor said . . . Bile ducts are working fine . . . and he held up the X-ray . . . And we don't need the catheter anymore, liver's working . . . And he rang for a nurse and she arrived with a tray of instruments and passed them to the doctor one by one, and he leaned over my husband and stitched and bandaged the catheter entry point, and when he was done he shook my husband's hand and said . . . Everything's going to be fine . . . And fine it was, relatively speaking, my husband got mashed potatoes for dinner, and as he ate wept at the luck . . .

And the next day my husband set off on his own, downstairs to the shop in the cafeteria, and once there he bought the biggest box of chocolates he could find, a gift for the nurses, to thank them for looking after him . . . But that box of chocolates weighed three and a half kilos, and so my husband only made it up one flight of stairs before he wiped out and the bonbons went flying, and he lay there on his back for a spell . . . and then he collected all the individually wrapped candy and asked one of the nurses heading upstairs to give him a hand with that box of chocolates, which he then gave the nursing staff as a gift . . .

And so the day came when I was to pick up my husband from the hospital, and they escorted him down to the car, my husband with his cane resembled a scarecrow, and it took him almost as long as Pavel to get into the car, and he sat beside me, a wretched little smile on his face . . . And when we pulled up to our forest parcel in Kersko I had to help him out of the car . . . and he stood there and it was just like an empty suit of clothes hanging there, and I had to get him his bicycle, all he wanted was his bicycle, and when I brought it over he stepped on the pedal and drove away on me, he got away on his bicycle, and then I took his things inside, and made his bed, and my husband pedaled by, he circled the car and away he went on his bicycle again, he was starting to return to form, running from me and running from himself, even running from that liver of his, running away on his bicycle from what he thought was cancer, because his liver still hurt . . . Then I helped him upstairs to his little attic room, and he collapsed into bed like he'd just been mountain climbing . . . And he said with a smile . . . When they discharged me, Doctor Štork says . . . You're healthy! And I say . . . And what about alcohol, Doctor? And he says . . . If you feel like it, go right ahead, here's to a glass of cognac! And I say . . . And what about coffee? And Docent Štork yells . . . Nurse! Bring us some coffee . . . And I say . . . And what about pilsner? And Docent Štork says . . . As soon as you leave the hospital you can head straight to Čížek's or the Black Brewery . . . You're healthy, but! You've got to watch what you eat, what works for you and what doesn't, it might just be that tea with lemon and a bread roll will make your bile ducts ache, while pork fat slathered on bread will set you right . . . and then my husband said to me . . . We wouldn't happen to have a slice of bread with some pork fat, would we? But after he ate that bread and pork fat he sat there listening to what it did to his insides, and presently this countrywoman from Semice stopped by, she'd had a gallbladder operation several years back, and she was keen to advise my husband on what he should and shouldn't eat, and she wept at her own plight, it was so many years since her operation, an operation performed, incidentally, by Emerich Polák himself, and still all she ate were digestive biscuits, and she was rewriting her last will and testament and it just broke her up, because she felt so sorry not just for her children and grandchildren but for herself as well . . . so said the countrywoman who came around on her bicycle to cheer up my husband, and then she cried for him as well, and my husband paled and staggered to the bathroom and vomited up that bread and pork fat . . . when he came back he was drenched in sweat, his face wet with sweat and tears, and he belched and burped and ran off again to the bathroom and you could hear him groaning into the toilet . . . and when he came back the countrywoman said . . . Bread slathered in pork fat, right? And my husband nodded and she just laughed and reached out and shook his hand and said . . .

There's two of us now in these here parts, two of us sentenced to die a gradual death of hunger, just like my mother . . . there's cancer in your family, right? And she looked him in the eye and he had to admit . . . My grandpa Tomáš died of cancer, as did my uncle Bob . . . And the countrywoman cried . . . That's it, then, it's hereditary! I'll come round and visit you, and vice versa, and we'll talk about the cancer and about the suffering, perhaps it's easier to face death when there's two of you . . . but look here, as a trade-off those of us who suffer from this disease have beautiful eyes . . . you yourself have such beautiful eyes . . .

Talking about your illness means diving back into it headfirst, my husband liked to say. And now that he was back from the hospital his favorite topic of conversation was his illness, he got to know everyone he could in Semice and Hradištko and Prague with a bad liver, he listened with pleasure to the litany of troubles, to the dietary constraints, listened with pleasure to women tell him how often they wept at their own fate, at the possibility they might die at any moment from complications of the liver. And so he listened to his own liver and felt sorry for himself, convinced it was only a matter of time until he was back in the hospital by Charles Square, he listened to anyone willing to share their post-op stories with him, and he listened to his liver and to his bile ducts, and he listened to those people prattle on about their diets, took pleasure in hearing that four years after their operations they still had problems, that as soon as they ate fat-slathered bread or a piece of fatty pork roast they had to lie down and contemplate the end. He loved the stories the nurses told, the things they'd seen, and the doctors too, who in addition to telling stories drew him diagrams of how his liver and gallbladder had worked in conjunction when he was still healthy . . .

. . . And then one day my husband just got up, it was like a change came over him, and when I brought him his tea with lemon he refused it, along with the bread roll, and he ordered me to go get a fresh loaf of bread and a pot of pork fat with crackling, and he slathered up a slice of bread and helped himself to the crackling, and a car pulled up at the gate and someone walked up the path, and my husband sat at the table eating his pork fat bread and crackling, and when that someone came in my husband offered her a bit of what he was eating, and she was most dismayed, because she wanted to talk about the operation, about the bile ducts, and I sat at the table working my new needlepoint, picking out yarn, and for some reason felt calmer than I had in a long time, my husband asked our guest to give him a ride to the butcher's in Přerov, he wanted to buy some pork chops and pork roast, because there was nothing better for your liver . . . And they returned with the chops and pork roast and that evening I made Wiener schnitzel and my husband made pork roast, and let it cool, and when his friends swung by, those friends who so loved talking about my husband's illness, he stopped them dead in their tracks by offering them cold pork roast and pouring himself a beer, and then he excused himself and hobbled out to his waiting bicycle, and he was off to his forest trails, his side roads, because when he was on his bicycle he could breathe like nowhere else, and the rhythmic breathing and the solitude brought him back to himself, allowed him to get a grip, no more obsessively weighing himself, no more feeling for his pulse, and one evening he came home scented with anise, he'd had a few shots of Prostějov rye in some pub, and that evening he slept like a baby . . .

While my husband was recovering, no matter where on earth he came back from on his bicycle, he always returned to that cottage in the Kersko forest elated, happy. And I was glad those forests and meadows and trails were doing him good, but in a week or so I noticed the aroma of rye liquor coming off him. And then I learned he had bottles of Prostějov rye strategically located all over the countryside, so that wherever he went he always came back from the forest tipsy, and happy. And he justified it with the academic Havránek's argument that the best thing for someone with a gallbladder just removed was pure liquor . . . My husband even had a visit from a former lieutenant colonel, who told him he'd had an operation a year ago and felt just fine now, but it wasn't always that way, he started out feeling awful, particularly when following a strict diet, until one day he was sitting around with his pals from the front, nursing a glass of mineral water while they knocked back vodka, and they convinced him to have a few, and he was pale and terrified what the booze would do to him, on edge what that liver of his was up to, but it just purred with delight and asked for more, more . . . And so the next afternoon when he was feeling surly and not himself again he asked his wife . . . Mother, go get me a bottle of vodka! And then he sipped at it as he was used to doing on the Eastern Front, and that evening he finally got a good night's sleep, after not sleeping for what seemed like ages, and he felt his insides relax, and his liver kick into full gear again, and so every day, as he was used to doing on the front, he drank a bottle of vodka, and he even got his appetite back, and his favorite was bread slathered in pork fat and bacon on the side.

. . . And so my husband toured the countryside on his bicycle, he had one bottle hidden away in an oak tree in The Giants, the forest past Přerov there, and he had one bottle hidden away in a hayloft all the way over on the Nymburk forest trail, and then a bottle in a haystack, and a bottle in the stream by Čepiček's Grove, where he loved to go because of the beautiful trail that ran alongside the River Labe, and he even had a bottle of Prostějov rye hidden as far away as Paleček, the hillside past Velenka, where the Mandšejd cemetery was, he kept that bottle behind the charnel house window, and he loved coming here, to Paleček, with its lovely view to the north, to Semity Heights, and White Mountain, he liked to lie here and gaze at the countryside, there was always a nice breeze, and my husband lay on the ground doing his breathing exercises, and then he liked to go into the cemetery and read the names and birthdays on the headstones, and when he discovered how many people younger than him were at rest here, he reached behind the window of the charnel house and drank to all those people who'd predeceased him, and then he continued on his way, or headed for home, but not before stopping for a drink somewhere in the Upper Kersko forest, taking a swig from a bottle hidden inside a hollow tree, and then he came home, bringing that elation along with him.

. . . And around this time my husband was friends with Mr. Kuzník, an elderly gentleman who cooked his own fruit slivovitz in a cottage back there on Nový meadow, and together he and my husband sat in the clearing in front of the Russian-style cottage, the sort Chekhov lived in, and Mr. Kuzník had an awful mess inside that cottage . . . his wife came out strictly on weekends, since she still worked, and she cooked up his food for the whole week and labeled all the pots, but Mr. Kuzník ate whichever one he happened to grab from the little cellar below the floor, and my husband was fond of going over there because Mr. Kuzník had dozens of bottles of moonshine in a lean-to out back, he had it categorized into the best, *Mittellauf,* the middling, *Vorlauf,* and the worst, *Nachlauf,* depending on how it had come out of the still . . . Mr. Kuzník had long since polished off the *Mittellauf,* and now that he and my husband were friends they were working on bottles of *Vorlauf* and *Nachlauf* together to cure their livers . . . Mr. Kuzník offered a bottle for my husband to sniff at, so as to determine what was still drinkable, and then they corked one bottle and swigged from another, depending on what they liked best, and thus they repaired their livers, because Mr. Kuzník's liver was kaput just like my husband's. Their main concern was to not go blind from the contents of those last few bottles, but they whittled them down, nostrils scorched from sniffing at them, until only one bottle was left, and even that one was drinkable, and so down she went . . .

Another thing my husband liked to do when in Kersko was frequent The Hunter's Blind every night, he sat here drinking beer with the local villagers, and when it was cold out they cooked up a jug of red wine. And here my husband was a number one, here he was king of central Europe, here they just couldn't get enough of him . . . and no matter where he was, pub or no, my husband never talked of his writing, or of what he suffered through for it, he never discussed literature, and if anyone asked him something related he just clammed up and stared at the table, played with his coaster, blushed and shrugged and said he didn't know what to say, everything he wanted to say was already in his books. What he did like talking about at the pub, however, was farm work, was *schweinfests,* was the lives of the villagers . . . and people came to The Hunter's Blind from Velenky, from Hradištko, from as far away as Semice, they pedaled in on their bicycles, old Premiers built back in the first republic, thirty, forty years old, and built to last forty more.

And one of the mainstays at The Hunter's Blind was Franta Vorel, who probably couldn't survive without this pub. Every day he was here at noon already, and then he took a bit of a breather before coming back in the evening, and Saturdays and Sundays he was here the whole day through. Franta most liked to sit next to the stove and quietly nurse his beer, and here and there a cup of coffee, but sometimes he just lost his mind and started downing shots of rum, and then he got dance fever and jumped up onto the tall stove, and danced up there until the soles of his shoes got hot, and then it was up onto a table, where he danced and kicked out his legs like the young Moravian dancers in their folk costumes. Franta was confidant to the barkeep and the barkeep's wife as well, with whom he'd always been in love. He brought her little gifts, and on busy nights he helped out at the taps, was honored to do so, and he always wore a clean white shirt and pulled those pints with a smile on his face . . . Franta was like an adviser to the barkeep, and when the frosts came he slept in the taproom and stoked the stove so the beer wouldn't freeze in the cellar.

. . . The barkeep's name was Novák and he had a beautiful wife indeed, and the snow fell and Christmas rolled around and Franta brought in some spruce trees, whatever the barkeep or his wife needed Franta showed up in his car and took care of . . . when Novák got the urge to cover the pub walls in oak paneling, it was Franta driving the oak logs to the sawmill in Poříčany, and when Novák thought of tiling the wall behind the stove, Franta took care of that too. But Franta's main thing was celebrating birthdays, not just his own, but his mother's, his daughter's, the barkeep's, the barkeep's wife's, and every one of Franta's guests toasted him most sincerely, and the wine and the liquor flowed, and Franta even provided a birthday cake with the celebrant's name on it, and those birthday parties at The Hunter's Blind inevitably ended up hosting all comers. About once a week I went to this pub to pass some time with the locals, sometimes there was a cottager or two come to check on their forest parcel, but during the week the regulars were mostly folks from the village, and they knew how to have a good time, now and then they brought in a couple of hares and the barkeep prepared them classic style, in a cream sauce, and once a month or so hunters even brought in a deer, and when it was cold out Mr. Hamáček or someone else brought *schweinfest* goodies, blood pudding and white pudding, and sausage, and as the guests and regulars of The Hunter's Blind waited out winter, more than once I overheard someone ask my husband, tactfully, and what did he plan on doing for his birthday?

. . . And while I continued to send entire print runs of books from the paper recycler's to the paper mills, I always did manage to divert several boxes of books, and the authors came around to pick up their few dozen copies and thank me and give me boxes of bonbons and that's how I came to know a number of writers in liquidation . . . my husband never lasted long out there in Kersko, he didn't know how to be home alone during the day, and so mornings he was on the bus to Prague, to visit his former magazine editors who were also in liquidation, and I always found it strange that my husband palled around with communists, but the sort of communists written off and drummed out of their editorial positions, out of their positions of confidence, right after those tank barrels were aimed at the Writers' Union and the academy and even the Pinkas pub . . . all these communists, friends of my husband's, now came out of the woodwork, and every one of them had the same look in his eye my husband did, fear . . . and when they smiled, it was the sort of smile that masks your tears. They stopped by my work to pick up books by Karl Teig, books by the philosopher Fischer, and by Egon Bondy, and books by Catholic poets published by Vyšehrad, also slated for the bin . . . my husband sent them around after spending the day with them at the Pinkas Pub, and even though the artillery piece was long gone from in front of Pinkas, that group of young people in liquidation whom the armies had come to quash that unhappy August were still in its sights. And so I invited all those writers and editors in liquidation to my husband's birthday party at The Hunter's Blind, on March 28, which according to the calendar was Teacher's Day, and the day Komenský was born . . . And they were thrilled at the invitation, moved to tears even . . . Are you serious, they said, Really? They didn't want to believe it, and one of them said that Smrkovský was just as poorly off, that he was abandoned, that he sat at home and no one wanted to talk to him, and if anyone deserved a little sympathy it was Smrkovský . . . And I said with a laugh . . . So he should come too! After all, my husband wrote a glowing article about him for the Agricultural News, he'd be pleased, he told me that Smrkovský hailed from Velenka, where he worked as a baker and attended communist meetings before the war.

. . . And so March 28 rolled around and there were Mr. Marysko and Břeťa and his wife too and at dusk we set off for The Hunter's Blind, and the barkeep and his wife were dressed to the nines, and they gave me a bouquet of flowers when we walked in, and Franta presented my husband with a giant birthday cake with chocolate lettering and a fondant rose . . . *To the Famous Writer . . . Happy Birthday* . . . And all the regulars were here, from Velenka, and Hradištko, and Semice, to party with my husband, and the whole pub was drowning in flowers and awash with light . . . and then two cars pulled up and a bunch of those writers and editors in liquidation piled out, and my husband invited them in and the painter Hegr unfurled a standard, a bed sheet on which was written . . . *Long Live Bohumil Hrabal, Famous Czech Scribe* . . . and the philosopher Kosík showed up too, and former secretary Kostroun, and even before they were seated they began to sing, and the barkeep and his wife went around pouring shots, which some people chased with beer, others with wine . . . and despite my husband's smile, he couldn't hide what he was thinking, that the gun aimed at the Writers' Union two years ago was now outside, invisible yet very real, aimed at The Hunter's Blind, and I was glad he was so dejected, but what, exactly, did he have to be afraid of? He should send them all to the devil, along with that gun of theirs, because, at the end of the day, what was so disturbing about his writing? And I sipped my drink and everyone was smiling, and Bartošek, that gorgeous man, stood on a chair conducting while everyone sang Moravian songs . . . and the doors flew open and there stood our former premier, Mr. Smrkovský . . . And he walked in and shook my husband's hand, congratulated him, he was impeccably dressed and he walked with a cane, and he went around and said hello to the other writers and editors in liquidation, and the barkeep shook his hand and then served us up Wiener schnitzel and potato salad . . . and Franta Vorel came over and shook hands with Smrkovský, and even Mr. Hamáček came over, who still lived just a few streets away from the house on the square where Smrkovský was born . . . And my husband was a little shaky, unsteady on his feet, he was putting back so much of the hard stuff, and he had this peculiar smile on his face . . . it just felt like all those people in liquidation sensed that invisible gun out in front of the pub, and they sang along together, and Hegr and Bartošek even raised that standard, that bedsheet, above my husband's head . . . *Long Live Bohumil Hrabal, Famous Czech Scribe* . . . And there on the table was the giant birthday cake with the chocolate lettering . . . *To the Famous Writer* . . . *Happy Birthday* . . . and now Mr. Smrkovský sat with Franta and Mr. Hamáček and inquired about who still lived in Velenka, and where, and how were they doing and how were their wives and kids . . . and now and then an editor or a writer stood up and shared a toast with my miserable husband, and then they toasted him again and again, because they all knew that something had to happen, that something was coming, they didn't know what, but they felt that gun aimed at the blazing windows of The Hunter's Blind, that gun standing somewhere in the dark of the oak trees . . . And I wasn't down, quite the contrary, I was happy that everything here at The Hunter's Blind was just the way it was, because now I saw that my husband was lying, he lied when he said his words and deeds would follow the truth, regardless of consequence, he lied to all his friends, those poets and painters he lectured at in Libeň, when he had the surroundings to say whatever he wanted, when they put back kegs of beer and mountains of pork tail, when he spoke of freedom and of how a writer, an artist, was immune to injury, because he was above all that . . . And of course he refused to speak to me about these things, I was just the one he threw Bible quotes at, depending on the situation . . . "But even the puppies eat the crumbs that fall from their masters' tables" . . . but I collected those crumbs well, so that I would remember them, and now as my husband fell apart from that gun he naively thought the armies had positioned just because of him, now I was confident in the knowledge that although I'd lost everything back in '45 and was locked up for half a year and made to work at the brickworks, I'd never fallen apart, never been afraid, because I was guilty of nothing . . . So give me a break, don't give me any of that crap! I lost a villa and a cottage and a factory and my own papa, who died because it was all too much for him . . . And now I sat here at The Hunter's Blind, sipping my drink and watching all these people in liquidation, who suffered not from guilt, but from terror, that's why they laughed and carried on so, why all the food and drink, why the singing, while I myself was suffused with calm, I'd never felt as calm as I did now, having invited all of them here so that no one would know who was coming, invited them here to the pub in the forest like Mrs. Agatha Christie might do with her own characters, before offing them, one by one . . .

. . . And Mr. Smrkovský, his chin resting on the handle of his silver cane, slowly took in the room, and then he rose from the table and said to my husband . . . Thank you, but I'm not in the best of health, I think I'll call it a night . . . and he shook hands with some of the villagers and waved to the rest of us, and then made his way outside, accompanied by former secretary Slavík . . . and Bartošek and Hegr the painter followed Mr. Smrkovský out, waving that bedsheet standard, and I went out too . . . and already there were cars turning in from Pramen Alley, and from the main road, high-beams on, three Volhas pulling up to The Hunter's Blind, and the car doors flew open and policemen in leather trench coats jumped out, followed by their commanding officer and men in civilian clothes, and there were cars from Prague, too, with purple police lights up top, and the policemen ran into The Hunter's Blind, fanned out as far back as the kitchen . . . and the men in the leather trench coats stood at every entrance and exit, in their pockets their revolvers at the ready . . . and two of them blocked the car Mr. Smrkovský sat in . . . And a tall man, apparently the head of the whole operation, stood dead center of The Hunter's Blind and said . . . Nothing to worry about, merely checking IDs . . . comrade commander, if you please . . . And the CO went from one person to the next, and it was dead quiet, smiles frozen on faces . . . and I thought my husband would collapse . . . The CO, in his uniform and pomaded hair, quietly collected everyone's ID, and took down their first and last names, their birthdates . . . Outside, two of the policemen seized and rolled up the bedsheet which read . . . *Long Live Bohumil Hrabal, Famous Czech Scribe* . . . and they brought it into The Hunter's Blind and handed it over to the CO and said . . . Smrkovský was greeted by these outrageous provocations . . . And the CO nodded and said . . . Bring it along as evidence . . . And I stood outside in the dark, through the open door I saw that whole group of editors and writers in liquidation, I could have left, but my husband sat there like he'd just had a heart attack . . . my husband was always afraid, but perhaps the only other time he'd been this scared out of his wits was when the SS grabbed him and took him for a ride on the locomotive, threatened to shoot him, and then kicked him off into the ditch, and now here we were, just a plain old ID check, a stupid review of our papers, the sort of thing that happened all the time on the bus and tram, and he was just as scared, even though the only reason this was happening was because they'd allowed themselves to be drawn here, en masse, like in a detective novel by Mrs. Agatha Christie . . . Only Mr. Marysko, whom I always suspected of being a little soft, stood his ground . . . When asked for his name he didn't even look up from his menu and said . . . It's written right there . . . And again the CO said . . . What's your name? And Marysko . . . If you can't read, have someone else read it for you . . . And the CO smirked and shook his head and took down the ID . . . And then the CO went outside and leaned into the car where Slavík and his wife waited and they handed him their IDs and answered his questions, even though all the information was right there in black and white, and when the CO asked who was in the backseat, Slavík said . . . that's Smrkovský, the former premier . . . and the CO clicked his heels together and looked carefully at Smrkovský, who leaned his head out the window . . . and the CO said . . . Comrade Smrkovský, your ID I don't need to see, I served under you back when you were still at the Ministry of Agriculture . . . you may go . . . And I walked into The Hunter's Blind, I wanted them to inspect my papers, I had my ID ready in hand, I wanted to make a crack like Mr. Marysko, but no one was interested in my ID . . . And then the CO barked an order and the men in the leather trench coats fanned out again, kitchen, hallway and cellar, and then they were outside, jumping into their cars, and the Volhas took off . . . and that was all she wrote for the birthday celebration . . .

. . . And one day it was pouring rain and three truckloads of *Buds* came in, it was raining all over them, I stood next to the scales and saw those bundled books, every one of them with my husband's name on it, and after weighing them in I drew up the consignment papers, weight, destination—one truck was going all the way to Holešov, two more to the paper mill in Štětí—and it poured rain, and I phoned my husband and presently he came down in the station wagon, and he stood there in the rain while I stood on the loading dock, and everyone saw how desolate he was there in the rain, even the boss, walking to the gate, turned around, and a clerk hopped down from the second truck and stood there in the rain looking at my husband, the laureate, who was soaked to the bone, like he fell in the river, and that clerk shrugged and said . . . It's not my fault, if it were up to me, I'd give you that whole truckload of *Buds* . . . And I said . . . But at least we can let him have one bundle . . .

And already that afternoon railway workers prowling the pubs on Letná had briefcases brimming with copies of *Buds,* stolen from box-cars, they were selling them for four pilsner beers, or twenty crowns apiece, and down at Forman's on Letná my husband bought ten copies for forty beers . . .

. . . And near the end of the month we drove to Moravia, and on the outskirts of Brno we were stopped at a checkpoint, and the police-man inspected my husband's ID, and out of nowhere he leaned in and said . . . So, Mr. Hrabal, have you come to pick up a few copies of *Buds*? Uh, no, said my husband, we're visiting friends . . . But the policeman handed back his ID and said with a laugh . . . Come on, you're on your way to pick up *Buds,* I already have my copy . . . They cleaned out a boxcar in Holešov and Brno is swamped with them . . .

My husband asked me very graciously if I wouldn't mind getting dressed up in my finest outfit, he wanted to take me along to So-jka's, since I knew German, but remember, I'd be representing our family's good name . . . And so I got all dolled up, and put on my makeup, and the minute we walked into Sojka's we were hit with such a wall of noise we had to yell at each other to be heard, and my husband rubbed his hands together and led me to a table marked RESERVÉ . . . and then he looked across the room, to where a hand-some older man with beautiful curly hair waved hello, he sat by the mirror, alone, fiddling with his own little RESERVÉ sign . . . and my husband went over to say hello to the man, whose whole demeanor indicated he was a gentleman, quite opposite to that barbarian of mine, and it was so loud in here conversation spilled from table to table, and my husband had to yell in the gentleman's ear . . . And when that jewel of mine came back our beer was already on the table, delivered by Jaruška, who'd been waiting tables here for ten years . . .

she smiled at my husband and he blushed, that was one of the nicest things about him, he still blushed when a pretty woman looked at him . . . What'll you have to eat, darling? she asked and my husband told her he'd signal her when it was time to bring out the Swedish cold cut tray he'd preordered . . . and then he was off on one of his stories, all the time looking across the room, to where that handsome gentleman sat by the cloakroom . . . That's Štastný, the translator, he translated all of what's-his-name's work, the American, damn it, it's slipped my mind . . . but you know him, he was here before the war . . . Mr. Štastný translated Erskine Caldwell too . . . And in September '38 Štastný showed Hemingway around town, and Hemingway sniffed around for a couple of days and said there'll be no war here . . . and off he went . . . Just take a look at him! When he was sixteen, Mr. Štastný, as an anarchist, tried to assassinate the prime minister and fled to America, and . . . here they come! My husband got up and walked over to a wretched-looking man, who was followed by a formidable-looking woman . . . And they said hello and my husband made the introductions and his friends had a seat and it was Heinrich Böll himself and his wife, and they told us they'd flown in from Moscow, where Heinrich, as chairman of Pen Club, had been to negotiate financial issues with respect to emigrants and the Moscow bureaucracy . . . And Jaruška brought over four beers and Mr. Böll, with those deep and beautiful eyes, looked at his glass with such sorrow that I knew it couldn't have been a cakewalk for his wife either, that jewel of hers probably had a shot liver too . . . and my husband raised his glass and shouted for everyone at our table to hear . . . To your health! And the next toast was for the Nobel Prize in Literature. And we drank our beer and my husband was already on his second while the laureate Mr. Heinrich Böll barely touched his, he did, however, empty a packet of powdered pills into his mouth, and his collar was sprinkled with white powder. And he said . . . My friends, I can only stay for half an hour, then I've got a meeting with the other writers . . . so, *mein lieber* Bohumil, how's the writing going, have you got the space to write? Any complaints? The thing is, I'm here officially, as chairman of Pen Club . . . And my husband yelled into Mr. Böll's ear . . . Of course I could complain, but I won't, because it wouldn't do any good anyway, I now belong to writers in liquidation . . . and so I write whatever I want, I have the luxury now of no holds barred . . .

you know what I mean? And Mr. Böll shouted . . . I do, even though I can barely hear myself think in here . . . so if you don't complain, then how about the others? With hundreds of writers not allowed to write, why no protest? And my husband shouted . . . I got protests, but I level them at myself because I'm yet to write a solid novel . . . and he added . . . Prometheus had to steal the fire for himself, no one's going to just give it to me . . . But Heinrich Böll persisted . . . But there are no literary magazines being published here, either professional or critical . . . and you're not being published either, right? And it was so loud at Sojka's my husband literally had to scream . . . No, I'm not being published, I now have the luxury of writing everything for the drawer again . . . and he helped himself from the tray brought round by Jaruška, and invited Mr. and Mrs. Böll to do the same . . . and Mrs. Böll set to with relish, as did I, while Mr. Böll only pecked at his ham and sipped at his beer . . . and Mrs. Böll, after she had a drink, said to me . . . The thing is, my dear, my husband isn't allowed to drink anymore, over the years he probably put back about ten cisterns of whiskey, he's got terrible cirrhosis and without the medicine he wouldn't even be around to see that Stockholm prize . . . And Heinrich Böll continued . . . So you really can't complain? And that's when I had enough and said . . . But Mr. Böll, it's not true, two of his books went to the pulp mill, he's not publishing, and on his birthday the police raided the pub there in the forest, and he says he can't complain? But my husband just laughed, and he wolfed down slices of ham and made like it was no big deal . . . True enough, but in this country it counts as publicity . . . I'm in the mix all the time, you yourself know that even in the West they write of me . . . *Une surprise dans la foret* . . . they sent me a news clipping from France about that birthday of mine . . . look, I can take it, I got thick skin by now . . . and like they say, what's cooked up at home gets eaten at home . . . you know that yourself, and here's one more . . . *Graecia capta, victorem cepit* . . . But whoever wants to protest, let them protest, myself I can't complain, well, maybe just at the pissoir . . . and my husband asked me to be sure to translate the last line, but Mr. Böll glanced at his watch and gave a start . . . We'll have to be going, they're expecting us at the Alcron . . . and my husband said . . . You're not going to finish your beer? and he pointed to the near full glass that Nobel laureate Heinrich Böll had barely touched . . . No more for me, Mr.

Böll said and he reached into his jacket again and withdrew his paper packet and tilted his head back and tapped the powdered medicine into his mouth, and then he brushed the white powder off his lapel and regarded my husband kindly, and I was so embarrassed, and he took my husband by the shoulders and feigned a kiss . . . *Mein lieber Bohumil, Sie sind ein redlicher Mann* . . . and my husband was so moved he picked up Mr. Böll's beer and downed it in one shot . . . And as we were saying our good-byes, Mrs. Böll offered my husband her hand and he kissed it, his lips wet with beer. Then my husband escorted his guests out to Belcred Street, and when he returned he said triumphantly . . . Now I remember the name of that American writer whose entire works Mr. Šťastný translated! Jack London! And my husband shouted so loud he drowned out the whole pub . . . It's nice when at least one member of our extended family is intelligent . . . ! And I shouted back . . . Thanks to booze! Except that precisely then the entire pub fell quiet and my voice cut through the smoke-filled air like a knife. And everyone turned to look at our table, at us, and once again my husband was number one, champion, and king of the world . . . And he raised a fresh glass of beer and guzzled it down like it was his first . . .

. . . And it came as a lifesaver, the letter from the housing ministry in Kobylisy informing us that our new flat in Sokolníky was ready, that we could pick up our keys and move into the flat I'd been making payments on for years, the high-rise flat that was little more than a blueprint a year ago. And the day came when we stood in front of the thirteen floor high-rise with a group of other prospective owners, and when it was our turn the clerks rode up with us in the elevator and unlocked the door to number 37, and then they wished us a happy future in this new flat of ours and off they went to the next one . . . And there we were in our new flat, and the sun shone in, and while my husband checked out the kitchen and the bedroom and the veranda with the great view of Prague, I couldn't get enough of the bathroom, and the separate WC, I even sat down on the toilet, it was warm here, and no draft blowing in like that WC back in Libeň, this was the greatest thing about living in a high-rise, fifteen years I'd waited to have my own bathroom, my own WC . . . And I depressed the handle and the water flushed, and I opened the hot and cold water taps in the bathroom and filled the tub, and I listened to the changing tone of the rising water and leaned over into the swirling steam, and I was happy, because all those years I'd dreamed of having my own bathroom and my own WC all under one roof . . . And we planned and drew diagrams where we were going to set up our furniture, the kitchen here was sixteen meters square, the living room eighteen, and the two bedrooms eleven and eight meters square . . . And then we drove back down to Libeň, from where my husband always insisted and carried on he would never, ever, move, and perhaps, if not for his operation, he would have stayed put in that flat on Na Hrázi Street, on the verge of immortality, as he liked to say, but that operation so weakened my husband, as did all the drinking with Mr. Kuzník, that ultimately even he agreed it was better to live in Sokolníky.

And so we turned in the keys to the landlady and stood here in the little courtyard one last time, we looked around in tears and during those few minutes I replayed my entire life here on Na Hrázi Street, all those in-house weddings, all those drinking binges, I saw all those people who used to visit us, all those passionate arguments, and I saw myself, in my white nightshirt, walking across the courtyard to the WC through the falling snow, I saw my husband up there on the roof, writing, fingers hammering away at the keyboard, I saw the places where he lay when he was too drunk to stand, and I opened the door to the washhouse and saw the old Swedish washing machine that once upon a time perforated all of our bedding, and I saw my husband and I moving our chairs around the courtyard, chasing the sun, and when it slipped beyond the courtyard even I went up to bask on the slanted, tarpaper roof, I saw that hallway with its peeling wet plaster and its whitewash, the narrow hallway from the street, where my husband always smudged his sleeves when he returned home from the pubs and stood there swaying . . . and I even saw that tabby cat of ours, Ethan, saw him waiting on us, and jumping through the narrow barred window to welcome us home, and I saw how much he loved us, and how much we loved that soaring, cat soul of his, and I saw that wild hanging ivy covering the walls and creeping along the wires my husband had strung up, and I even saw that death mask still hanging here, girdled by tendrils of wild ivy, the death mask Mr. Boudník made of my husband . . . I stood here dazzled by those images I thought were long gone and buried in the past, I stood here in the little courtyard and plain as day could recount that life of mine, from the moment I first set foot here and saw that man through the open twilit window washing floors, that man who was to be my husband, I saw myself in those days before we met, as the woman who had wanted to commit suicide, but once I was with my husband I had neither the time nor the inclination for such thoughts, for over the years my husband had so engaged me, frustrated and enraged me, that I even forgot to have a child of my own, my husband was enough of a handful . . . I shrugged, what can you do? In tears I ran down the stairs, to smudge my sleeves on the peeling walls one last time . . .

October–November–December 1985

■ □ ■ □ ■

WRITINGS FROM AN UNBOUND EUROPE

For a complete list of titles, visit www.nupress.northwestern.edu.

Words Are Something Else
DAVID ALBAHARI

Perverzion
YURI ANDRUKHOVYCH

The Second Book
MUHAREM BAZDULJ

Tworki
MAREK BIEŃCZYK

The Grand Prize and Other Stories
DANIELA CRĂSNARU

Peltse and Pentameron
VOLODYMYR DIBROVA

And Other Stories
GEORGI GOSPODINOV

The Tango Player
CHRISTOPH HEIN

In-House Weddings
BOHUMIL HRABAL

Mocking Desire
DRAGO JANČAR

A Land the Size of Binoculars
IGOR KLEKH

Balkan Blues: Writing Out of Yugoslavia
EDITED BY JOANNA LABON

The Loss
VLADIMIR MAKANIN

Compulsory Happiness
NORMAN MANEA

Border State
TÕNU ÕNNEPALU

How to Quiet a Vampire: A Sotie
BORISLAV PEKIĆ

A Voice: Selected Poems
ANZHELINA POLONSKAYA

Estonian Short Stories
EDITED BY KAJAR PRUUL AND DARLENE REDDAWAY

The Third Shore: Women's Fiction from East Central Europe
EDITED BY AGATA SCHWARTZ AND LUISE VON FLOTOW

Death and the Dervish
The Fortress
MEŠA SELIMOVIĆ

The Last Journey of Ago Ymeri
BASHKIM SHEHU

Conversation with Spinoza: A Cobweb Novel
GOCE SMILEVSKI

House of Day, House of Night
OLGA TOKARCZUK

Materada
FULVIO TOMIZZA

Shamara and Other Stories
SVETLANA VASILENKO

Lodgers
NENAD VELIČKOVIĆ